THE DOG FOOD MYSTERY

N.F. WOLFE

ISBN 979-8-88851-453-5 (Paperback)
ISBN 979-8-88851-454-2 (Digital)

Copyright © 2023 N.F. Wolfe
All rights reserved
First Edition

All rights reserved. No part of this publication may be reproduced, distributed, or transmitted in any form or by any means, including photocopying, recording, or other electronic or mechanical methods without the prior written permission of the publisher. For permission requests, solicit the publisher via the address below.

Covenant Books
11661 Hwy 707
Murrells Inlet, SC 29576
www.covenantbooks.com

CHAPTER 1

The streetlight on the sidewalk shone a soft light into her bedroom, just enough so that she did not need a night-light. Shannon Parker lay in her bed, looking at the shadows that it cast on her wall. Suddenly, a bright light from the motion-activated spotlight across the street filled the room. As she sprang from her bed, she saw a shadow of someone running away amid the sounds of a barking dog. She tried to follow the figure, but it disappeared into the darkness. Chaos ensued. Dogs barking, lights blinking on, police sirens responding to the prowler call.

"Well, did you hear all the commotion last night?" Mom asked as Shannon bounded down the stairs for breakfast.

"I saw the spotlight from the Harrisons' house when it came on and a person run from their carport. Did the police find anything?" she responded.

"No, the only thing that was disturbed was a bag of dog food that was not in the usual place, but, otherwise, everything was as it should have been, no broken car windows, nothing else disturbed. But you say you saw someone running from the carport. Could you tell who it was?" asked Mom.

"It was only a shadow that ran in front of the spotlight in the flower bed. I couldn't tell who it was," she said.

Dad joined in on the conversation as he came around the corner into the kitchen. "You know, it seems to me that I heard there have been other recent similar incidents in areas close to ours. No forced entry, and nothing missing. Seems like I remember that the only thing that was disturbed was a bag of dog food, and even that was not stolen, just disturbed. Guess we can call this the 'dog food caper,'" he joked.

Mom frowned at him. "Well, you can laugh if you want, Todd Parker, but it is frightening to me that a stranger could be that close in your carport or garage. It poses a threat in my mind that maybe it is just testing the waters to see how close he can get. May lead to something more serious next time."

"I see your point," he said in a more serious tone. "But how do you know it was a 'he'? Shannon, could you tell if it was a male or a female?"

"No, Dad. Like I said, it was only a shadow running across the light," she said.

"What was running across what light?" asked fourteen-year-old Rudy as he rounded the corner to the breakfast nook, his blond hair still in disarray from sleeping and his blue eyes barely awake.

"If you were ever on time for breakfast, you would know what," laughed Mom. "Sit down, and we will fill you in on what you missed, sleepyhead."

After breakfast, Shannon and Rudy rushed off to catch the bus for Eastwood High School. The sun was just starting to peek over the horizon. Sixteen-year-old Clarissa Flores and her younger sister, fifteen-year-old Elena, were already at the bus stop. "Hola," said Shannon.

"Hey, girl. You still pretending you can speak Spanish," laughed Clarissa.

"Well, I keep trying to learn, but my brain cannot think as fast as you guys can talk," replied Shannon.

"Anyone who can process engineering and robotics should certainly be able to learn a new language," said Clarissa.

"Maybe that is the problem. I can't translate that technology into Spanish, so I continue to think in English," Shannon surmised.

"Good point," said Clarissa. "Here comes the bus and Alejandro is not here. That boy is always late. How he ever gets to football practice on time is a mystery."

Rudy laughed. "Well, he doesn't always get there on time. Why do you think he is so fast? All those extra laps for being late. Here he comes now."

Fourteen-year-old Alejandro bounded down the sidewalk and hopped on the bus. The others boarded behind him, laughing at his pretense of urgency.

As the bus rolled along the 375 Loop, the lights from Ciudad Juarez could be seen in the distance. Shannon and Rudy had visited there with Mom and Dad when they were younger. Shannon's favorite sites were the Cathedral of our Lady Guadalupe on Plaza de Armas and the art, technology, and space exhibits at the museum La Rodadora Interactive Space. That visit piqued her interest in technology, which led to her parents selecting Eastwood for her and Rudy's high school years. Rudy excelled on the football team as a running back, and Shannon enrolled in Engineering and Robotics and was also able to further her musical interests in the band while maintaining a 3.9 GPA.

"Elena, did you hear about the prowler last night?" Rudy asked.

"I heard the sirens and the dogs barking. What was it all about?" asked Elena as the bus pulled onto the school parking lot.

"I'll tell you all about it on our way to class," he said.

The day went by pretty fast for Shannon, except for literature, which was her least favorite subject. After school, she reported to the band room for band practice, and Rudy to the football field for football practice.

Eastwood High required all students to take music all four years of high school. It was the opinion of the school administration that students who were involved in music tended to do better academically. All students were required to take orchestral music, and the more *talented* were recruited for the marching band and color guard.

The football team was, of course, exempted from the marching band, but not from orchestral band. Participation in marching band required tryouts as the band travelled to competitions and had earned top ratings among bands at schools of like size. Because of the COVID-19 shutdowns, there was only remote learning for much of the previous school year. Activities like sports and music, including marching band, were suspended. It was good to be back in school with friends.

Shannon tried out for marching band because Dad and Mr. Flores, Clarissa's dad, alternated picking up Shannon, Clarissa, Rudy, Alejandro, and Elena, which made it convenient for all to participate in the extracurricular activities.

Shannon played the xylophone, which was in the "pit," meaning she did not have to learn the marching drill. With her demanding academic studies, she didn't need any more distractions. She could learn and excel at the musical pieces, which were extremely hard, with time signatures that most people did not understand. Mr. Mansion always selected very difficult music. He knew that a well-performed difficult program would earn higher scores than a simple one.

Clarissa waved to Shannon as she entered the room carrying the flag and rifle, items she used during the performances. "How was school today?" she asked Shannon.

"Good," she replied. "There is a new boy in the E&R class. No one knows him, and he apparently has transferred from another school here in the city. I didn't get a chance to introduce myself. He seems nice, kinda quiet and really cute."

Mr. Mansion took control of the room, and a noise wafted out of the band room in semi-melodic fashion—this being the first time the students were introduced to the new music.

It was Mr. Flores's day to pick up the *kids*, and, being a little early, he watched as the band members, who had now come onto the practice field, were introduced to their places for the marching drill. Shannon was in the "pit," with really nothing to do as the music was so new. She was so stately, standing behind her instrument, tall and slim, with flowing honey blond hair just below her shoulders. Although he could not see them from the stands, he knew that her light complexion and piercing blue eyes projected wisdom beyond her years. It was almost as though Shannon could see into your soul.

As he found his daughter, Clarissa, he noted the contrast. Clarissa was a bit shorter, but not much, with dark brown hair, dark complexion, and brown eyes. Clarissa always had a smile for everyone she met and could light up a room just by walking into it. She loved to joke and kept most conversations moving in a happy direction.

Band and football practice over, Mr. Flores delivered Shannon and Rudy to their driveway. The aromas from "supper on the stove" were a welcome sensation to the siblings as they entered the front door. As Shannon ravaged her dinner, she commented that the tomatoes were particularly good. "These must be homegrown from your garden, Mom," she said.

"Yes, they are," Mom said proudly. "But it's funny. I thought I had more tomatoes on the vines when I checked yesterday. The netting around the garden has not been disturbed, but it looks as though several are missing. You would think an animal raiding the garden would displace the netting."

"Unless they are really smart animals," laughed Rudy.

"Well," said Mom, "I don't know how, but I wondered if it could be related to the prowler incidences."

"Well, I talked with Johnny Cooper today," said Todd. Johnny, a friend of Todd's and Debra's and a police officer in the precinct serving the Parker's community, had been investigating the disturbances. "He says these reports are coming from people living close to us. None of them would indicate a serious problem, mostly little things that are just dislocated, nothing missing. The police have been unable to find any evidence that would lead them to whoever or whatever is responsible for these incidences."

"I am still unsettled about all of this," said Debra as she began to clear the table.

"I will get the dishes, Mom," said Shannon.

"Thanks, Shannon," said Mom, "but you and Rudy get to your homework. I know both of you are tired. I will get these. I may even get Dad to help," she laughed.

That was Dad's cue to hastily exit the room.

CHAPTER 2

It was late Saturday afternoon, and the sign on the door said "Come around back." Todd, Debra, Shannon, and Rudy knew that before they approached the door and headed for the backyard. The Flores family chose to host the third quarter block party every year, and it was always a huge success. They selected the third quarter because July can be brutally hot in El Paso, and their backyard is tricked out with a covered patio/deck, comfortable lawn furniture, a ceiling fan, and a misting area—a welcome relief from the heat.

Roberto (Bob) and Cindy welcomed the Parkers with a drink in hand and lead them to the buffet table, where Debra deposited her Mexican corn casserole before joining the other guests: the Andersons, the Gaithers, the Roberts, the Harrisons, and another family whom they had not met. Shannon guessed who they were right away when she saw the new boy in E&R class. He was a handsome young man, tall for his age, sandy hair, sad dark brown eyes that shown like black pearls, and a muscular build.

"Debra, Todd, Shannon, Rudy Parker, meet Allison and William Jeffries and their son, Bill," said Cindy. "They just moved into the neighborhood two weeks ago. I believe Bill is going to school with you and Rudy, Shannon," she continued.

"Yes, I saw you in my Engineering and Robotics class," Shannon said to Bill. "How are you liking school so far?"

"It is different from my last school. Lots of opportunities for studies that are not offered there. I am excited about the E&R class, just tolerating other studies," he laughed.

"I know what you mean. Wish I could opt out of literature. I have no idea what the 'deeper' meaning of a poem is. Just thought that was a forest on a snowy morning," she quipped. "I guess you are enrolled in music. Everyone has to be. Are you trying out for marching band?"

"Although I took music at my old school, the school was small, and there were not enough band members to comprise a marching band, so I have not made a decision about trying out. I know that Eastwood has an excellent marching band. Not sure I would be good enough," he said.

"You should try out. Dr. Mansion is an excellent band instructor, and I think you would enjoy the 'family' atmosphere of the marching band and color guard parents and students," said Shannon. "Those band competition trips are so much fun once we get over the jitters of competing."

Bill grinned, his pearly white teeth beautiful against his tanned face. "I have an after-school job and, if I can work the schedule around practice, I may just do that," he said.

Clarissa told everyone to come and help their plates, and the feast was on. After dinner, the youngsters started playing a game of frisbee, the teenagers drifted off to talk about school and other such teenage things, and the adults migrated to the misting area. Sitting under the mister and enjoying a respite from the heat, the Jeffries were brought up to speed on the "prowler" issue.

Todd mentioned that Shannon had seen the shadow of the prowler at the Harrisons' but couldn't tell who it was. Hannah Anderson told the group that they, too, had noticed unusual activity at their house. Nothing missing that she noticed, just things slightly ajar from their normal place. Fred Gaither said they had noticed the same, and Betty Roberts said she is noticing that vegetables from her garden seem to be missing.

"At first," she said, "I thought it was an animal, but when I was preparing to make my hot pepper jelly, I noticed that I barely had enough peppers. A week ago, there were scads of peppers on those plants. I don't know of any animal that would eat hot peppers."

Todd told the group about his conversation with Johnny Cooper at the police department and said they were increasing patrols in the area in hopes of discovering who or what this was.

"Since there has been no intrusion, theft, or obvious damage to property, we are all hoping it is harmless," he said. "But Debra makes a good point that we don't know if this is the prelude to something more dangerous. Let's all be on our guard and report to the police and each other anything we see or suspect that is out of the ordinary. I would rather report something insignificant than ignore it and have something more sinister happen."

By dessert time, the conversation changed to sharing cookout recipes, the local election, zoning changes, repairs needed for the street, and other such issues. And it wouldn't be a good get together in Texas without a long dissertation from someone about how the Dallas Cowboys are going to do this fall. George Roberts provided that.

As the sun receded behind the horizon, the photocell lights took over, and the group started to wind down their conversations. The young children were getting tired, and the teenagers, ever energetic, reluctantly broke up their meeting and readied to leave.

"Hey, see you all Monday," said Shannon as she and her family walked from the backyard.

"Yeah, see ya," all the others, except Bill, chimed in.

Shannon had noticed that all during the get-together, he had remained very quiet, even after they broke up into groups. There was an aura about him as though he had some sadness in his life, but she could not imagine what it would be. His mom and dad seemed very nice. The three of them had come to the party, so she assumed that he had no siblings. But she also knew that one cannot possibly know what a person was feeling without knowing them better. She hoped to do just that and decided on the way home that Monday she would begin that journey.

When they arrived home, Todd mentioned what a good time was had by all. Shannon asked how he liked the new family. Todd said, "They are a strong, Christian family who have had more than their share of bad knocks. Their ten-year-old son drowned in their pool, which is one of the reasons they moved. William said it was just too painful to live in a house where such tragic memories flooded over you every time you passed his room or looked in the backyard. And Bill found it difficult to even go into the backyard. Bill and his brother were very close. To make things worse, Bill and his brother were both in the pool when Bill got out to make a phone call to his girlfriend. When he turned around, his brother had disappeared beneath the surface, and even though Bill immediately jumped in to save him, it was too late. Bill cannot get over feeling that he is responsible and even stopped dating the girl he felt he had abandoned his brother to call."

Shannon almost wished she could unhear that conversation. She was afraid that Bill would be able to see how sorry she felt for him. She knew that would drive him away, and she wanted to start a friendship that was based on positive emotions and feelings, not pity, and, obviously, he needed a good friend.

"He said he has an after-school job," she changed the subject. "Do you know what he does?"

"William said Bill is a go-getter, working to save for college. He works for a landscape company. Hard job, especially in this area of the country," said Todd.

"Dad," she asked, "don't you think it is time for me to get a job? I can work on Saturday and after school except during band season."

"Where are you thinking of applying?" he asked.

"I had not really thought much about it," she replied. "Restaurant, grocery store, clothing boutique. I don't really know who would be hiring right now. What do you think?"

"Let me think about it, Shannon," he said. "My concerns are that you may see your grades fall, and you know how important it is to keep your GPA up if you want to get into a good college. But I know you will do what you need to do to keep your grades up. More than that, I worry about safety. With crime increasing, the first targets would be fast-food restaurants. Grocery stores may be safer, especially if you work stocking shelves rather than as a cashier. And the smash and grabs usually hit drug stores and retail stores. I'm not sure the smaller boutiques would be immune from them."

"But, Dad," she said, "at some point, I have to be willing to take that chance and live my life."

"Yes, baby," Dad said, "but, as a parent, I need to keep you safe as long as I can. Your chosen profession in research and development in robotics, should you not change your mind, will be a safer place to begin your working career. Let me think about it. I may say I am so proud of you for wanting to work. Just know that your mother and I both feel that you are 'working' hard enough with all of the course study you have and the extracurricular activities."

"I love you, Dad," said Shannon. "Just think about it."

"I love you too, baby," said Dad. "I will."

CHAPTER 3

Breakfast at the Parker house was very special on Sundays. Today, it was sausage, cheese omelets, sweet rolls, and fruit. Mom served breakfast with a twinkle in her eye. "Guess who's coming to dinner and staying for two weeks," she said.

"Not much of a mystery there," said Shannon. "You only get this excited about one person, Aunt Francie." Aunt Francie, born Francesca, was dubbed Aunt Francie because the children could not pronounce her name, and thus, *Francie* stuck. "How did she get away from her job long enough to stay for two weeks?"

"Well, she actually will be working part of the time. Because of the immigration issues here along the border, the Department of Homeland Security thought they could better utilize her time and expertise here rather than in Washington."

Regardless of the reason she was coming, Shannon, Rudy, and Todd were all thinking about the endless pasta bowls, salads, and all of the other Italian fare that she cooked when she stayed with them. Born to Italian immigrants, she and Debra both loved to cook, but when Francie came to visit, she would literally run Debra out of the kitchen. Although she protested, it was a welcomed relief for Mom.

Francesca was an immigration analyst with the Department of Homeland Security's US Citizenship and Immigration Services when she met John Stricker, a Secret Service agent fifteen years ago. She was five feet six inches tall with jet black hair, slightly built with big brown eyes set in a beautiful olive complexion. She was kind and generous, which, aside from her beauty, was one of the things that attracted John. John was a fair-haired, five-feet-eleven-inch *muscular* man with alert hazel eyes, taking in everything around him. It didn't take either of them long to fall in love and were married a year later in a small but beautiful wedding at the UMD Memorial Chapel in College Park, Maryland. They settled down in a moderate-sized home in Germantown, Maryland, because it was less than an hour's commute to DC. It was only later that they found out their town was the place where George Atzerodt, a coconspirator in the assassination of President Abraham Lincoln, was captured.

They lived happily for ten years, adapting to the demands of each other's career. John would be gone for days at a time when traveling with the president. After three years with the department, Francie was promoted to immigration officer. She worked from home some of the time as her position required research and analysis that could be done remotely. John and Francie were not blessed with children, but both were so involved with their different careers that they were fulfilled by indulging Shannon and Rudy when they were able to visit. Francie would sometimes come to visit while John was travelling.

It was on one of these visits that the call came from *Washington* that John had been involved in an explosion in *France*. The president was scheduled to visit, and John was on the advance task force to clear the route to the hotel where the president would be traveling the following day. A terrorist had planted a remote detonated car bomb that blew up prematurely. John was badly injured and flown back to the hospital in Washington.

Francie booked the next plane back to DC, where she found John still in a coma and badly injured. He finally came out of the coma a month later. His injuries were limited to a concussion and burns on his body, and he, fortunately, did not lose any limbs. But the journey back to health would require months, maybe years, of physical therapy as well as counseling for PTSD. It was highly unlikely he would be able to return to his position with the Secret Service.

That was five years ago, and finally, he was cleared to return to the Secret Service but in a different role—one that did not require in person exposure to the dangers that those brave agents face. His was more geared to analysis and reporting of data.

Francie arrived midafternoon with bags of clothes and gifts for the kids. After unpacking and catching up with the family, her first stop was inspection of the kitchen. Of course, there would be some shopping that had to be done. Debra laughed and made the grocery list.

After dinner, which Debra cooked, they all retired to the covered front porch to relax and enjoy the sound of the gentle rain that had started to fall, cooling the August evening.

"Well, Debra," said Francie, "I will have to admit I could get used to some good Tex-Mex cooking. I may have to carry some of your recipes back to Maryland with me. I am sure John gets tired of Italian."

"I am glad to share with you," said Debra. "Better yet, you and John make some time to come on down for an extended visit, and I'll do the cooking," she laughed.

"How is John dealing with his new position?" asked Todd.

"At first, he felt useless because he was not on the front lines," replied Francie. "But he has come to realize that the work he is doing helps to keep the agents out there safe. More than a few times, the intel he has gathered has altered the course of action preventing a catastrophic outcome. We are traveling a bit more as he is becoming more comfortable. The PTSD as an aftermath of the bomb is a major factor in his reluctance to go out.

"Luckily," she continued, "treatment for the PTSD was strongly encouraged by the physical therapist, a young man that John came to hold in high regard. He was in denial about the PTSD at first, thinking that it was a sign of weakness. With the guidance of the therapist, he came to realize that he had no control over it. He started to talk to me about how he felt, and as we would discuss his feelings and fears and as he continued with counseling, trust started to build, and his episodes became more infrequent and not as severe. You know," she said pensively, "each person processes trauma differently. The tragedy is that trauma comes in different ways as well. It could be a bomb, as in John's case, or the loss of a family member or friend, or physical or mental abuse. It sometimes goes unrecognized unless it is caused by a traumatic event. But we know that the mind is resilient and, with help, can recover. At one point, I feared he would become a total recluse, but gradually, he is venturing out, especially with me."

"Frankly," Todd responded, "John is not the only one who is concerned these days with venturing out because of safety issues. More and more we hear of everyday people doing everyday things that get caught up in horrible circumstances because of some deranged person or persons."

Rudy said, "There is someone who is roaming the neighborhood at night. It makes me scared to go outside after dark."

"What do the police say?" asked Francie.

"At this point," Todd replied, "there isn't any evidence that this is a dangerous situation as there have been no break-ins, no damaged property, and no assaults. None of us knows what to think. At first, we thought it might be an animal, racoon, or something," he continued. "Shannon is the only one who has seen the person, and then it was only a shadow. So we know that it is definitely not an animal."

"That is frightening," said Francie, "in view of the coyotes operating on the border. I assume the police are patrolling frequently."

"Yes," said Todd. "They have stepped up the patrols and have asked the neighborhood to report the slightest thing."

As the rain turned into a downpour, the group moved inside and said their "good nights." Francie wondered if the events developing in this neighborhood would have any bearing on the reason she had been sent to El Paso.

CHAPTER 4

The days were getting shorter and cooler in South Texas. On evenings like this, Shannon enjoyed sitting in the front porch swing, listening to the sounds of the night—crickets, an owl in the distance, a few birds gathering that final worm for the babies. A peaceful sensation flowed over her as she closed her eyes to better take in the atmosphere.

She was startled when she heard footsteps coming up the walkway to the house. "Who is there?" she asked.

"Hi, Shannon. It's me, Bill," he said as his face was illuminated by the motion-activated porch light. "I was just out for a walk to think through a few things." he said. "Thought we could talk a bit if you have time."

"Sure, Bill," said Shannon. "Come sit down."

Bill sat in a chair opposite the swing. For several minutes he did not say a word, looking pained and conflicted.

"Bill, I don't know what is bothering you, but I want to listen and help you sort through whatever it is," said Shannon.

Bill looked down for several minutes and then raised his eyes to meet Shannon's. "Shannon, you may not know why we moved from our old neighborhood," he said. "There was a terrible accident, and we just couldn't live there any longer."

Shannon didn't say anything, waiting on Bill to continue.

"My brother drowned in our swimming pool, and, for a while, everyone, including myself, blamed me. I could tell that Mom and Dad, although they love me, felt I was responsible for not being where I should have been to rescue Jake. I had stepped out of the pool to call a girl, and in that minute or two, he just disappeared from the surface. By the time I pulled him out, he was gone. Paramedics could not bring him back," he said as tears began to fall. "It was only after the medical examiner told us that Jake had apparently had a seizure that some of the guilt subsided. Still, if I had not left the pool, Jake would be alive today. Surely, I could have heard him struggling. Shannon, Jake was not only my brother. He was my best friend. How can I ever forgive myself for the loss to my family and myself that Jake's death caused? Even my friends, mostly their parents, distanced themselves from me and my parents. I didn't want to go to school or go out socially. I was so lost and lonely. That was two years ago, and, to compound things, I failed my freshman year."

"Bill, had Jake ever had a seizure before?" asked Shannon.

"The medical examiner said there was evidence that he may have had previous seizures, but we never saw him have one," said Bill.

"You know, Bill," said Shannon, "I am not a medical expert, but I have read that some seizures are not what we would think of as a seizure like writhing and convulsing. Some are just quiet moments in which the person seems to be disconnected, for lack of a better description."

Bill looked pensive for a moment. "We used to say Jake was 'zoning' again," responded Bill. "Usually, after a minute or two, he would look at us, and we would all laugh. Do you think that could have been a seizure?"

"I would say it is entirely possible," said Shannon. "And if that is so, had you been right beside him in the pool, you may not have known he was unconscious and drowning until it was too late."

"Still, I was angry at myself and then angry at my parents for not speaking up for me with the teachers. Having to repeat the ninth grade was so humiliating. You would not understand what it is like to fail," he said.

"Bill," Shannon said, "because of my birthday, I was always the youngest person in my class. I almost failed in grade school and was saved only by having tutoring through the summer. Yes, I was given a provisional pass, and, yes, I went on to excel in my studies, but only with exceptionally hard work. Mom has frequently said as I struggled with school assignments and exams that she thinks repeating that grade would have been the wisest thing. She felt that it was not my intellect, but my level of maturity that held me back. I believe that she was right."

"You put a lot of faith in your mother's advice, don't you, Shannon?" asked Bill.

"You know, Bill," Shannon responded, "once, she said to Rudy and me, 'I have been where you are, but you have never been where I am. The wisdom and understanding that comes with living longer gives you a different perspective. Perhaps I can see and have gone through things that you have not yet encountered. Accepting advice from someone of experience may avoid heartaches for you.'"

They sat quietly for several more minutes before Bill said, "I guess I had better get back. I didn't tell Mom and Dad I was going out. Shannon, thank you for listening. You have given me hope that this guilt will not last forever."

Shannon said, "Bill, I have two good ears, and they will always be open to you if you want to talk about anything."

Bill stood, bent over, and kissed Shannon on the cheek, turned and walked away. After a few minutes, the porch light went out, and Shannon was left in the dark to think about the pain Bill and his family had endured for the last two years. She hoped that, with the help of their new friends, they would find hope for a happier future.

CHAPTER 5

The noise woke the whole house. Shannon, her parents, Rudy, and Aunt Francie all met in the hall at the same time. "What was that?" asked Rudy, a frightened look on his face.

"Not sure," said Dad as he rushed down the stairs.

"It came from around the back of the house," said Shannon, close on Dad's heels.

"Well, whatever it was, it tripped the back porch light and the trash can is overturned," said Dad as he bounded out the back door. "Did you hear anything else?" he asked Shannon.

"The only thing I remember hearing was the next-door neighbor's dog barking. Mr. Taylor must have let him out for a bathroom break. But I just thought he had seen some animal invading his space," said Shannon.

"Well, it could just be a racoon raiding the garbage can. Still, it would have been a *big* racoon to uncover and overturn this trash can," Todd said. "Whatever it was, it is gone now. Back to bed, everyone."

Having such a start, it was difficult to get back to sleep, and Shannon lay awake thinking about what happened tonight. She remembered the episode across the street a week ago and wondered if the two could be related. What, or who, is disturbing dog food bags and trash cans? Could Mom be right—this is only a test? If that is true, either this "thief" is very clumsy or trying to get people so accustomed to these incidents that they ignore the intrusions.

When dawn broke, she had just dozed off, and the sunlight streaming through her window awakened her. She showered and dressed, still pondering what was going on in their neighborhood.

Mom had cooked blueberry pancakes, her favorite. When Rudy and Dad came down to breakfast, Dad said he had just made a call to Johnny, his close friend at the police department. He said he had told him about the incident last night.

"Johnny said that they have had several more reports of other similar incidents, all within a close proximity to this neighborhood. He said that, at first, it seemed that these nocturnal visits may be animals, but as more of them were reported, concern began to grow that something else was afoot. Although they have stepped up patrols, they have been unable to catch the person and have no leads in the case," Dad explained.

"I think, Debra, that Johnny is thinking along the lines that you are," Dad said to Mom. "This may be a test to see who is home and even how secure the home may be before breaking in. There may even be more than one person involved if that is the case."

"What I don't understand," said Shannon, "is with as many 'yard dogs' as we have around us, why the entire neighborhood is not roused by their barking. Do you think they are being doped?"

"That is a good observation and one that would be truly terrifying if it is the case," said Dad. "It would show a great deal of sophistication and mal intent. I think I will mount my trail camera out back to see what we can pick up on it. I will also talk to our neighbors and let them know that any measures they can take to record trespassers will be advisable. Being Saturday, most of them are home, and frankly, I think this a matter of urgency, so much so that the police department will be cruising this area and those around us until this culprit can be discovered, animal or human."

After breakfast, Shannon offered to make sure that all of the trash was back securely in the trash can. As she gathered articles that Dad had missed in the dark last night, she noticed what looked like a trail of trash leading into the woods behind the house, one of the very rare wooded areas in El Paso. She and Rudy used to play in those woods and even had a tree house when they were younger. At sixteen, Shannon had not visited the tree house in years, and Rudy lost interest when he started playing sports.

As she entered the woods, she noticed footprints on the dirt path that was still there after all those years. Although weeds were encroaching on the path, it was still visible as though it were still being used. Since the woods were on their property and there were houses on the back side of the property, she wondered who might be using this path. The only access to the woods was over a high fence or through their backyard. A shiver ran over her as she pondered the implications of someone being that close to them without their knowledge.

She was still seeing an occasional piece of trash beside the path as she cautiously inched her way into the woods. She recognized one of the items as an expired frozen dinner that Mom had thrown out yesterday. She was getting close to the place where their tree house had been, sure that it had long since fallen down. But there it was, still in the tree, although a bit worse for the wear. The ladder looked sturdy enough, and she started to climb, being careful that each step could support her weight.

Looking into the tree house, it appeared to her that someone was living here. There were newspapers and remnants of food and even dog food. This had to be the source of the clandestine visits to carports and trash cans. But who could be living here and why and how did he, or she, find the tree house and where is he now? As she pondered all these questions, it occurred to her that whoever this was would surely not escalate to breaking and entering or other crimes. This looked like a squatter, down on his luck, who had found a place to hide from the world. She questioned whether she should tell the police or even her parents. Since it was Saturday and she had no place to go, she decided to "stake out" the place and see if the trespasser would return.

Finding one of the "hiding" places that she and Rudy used when they were little, she settled in to watch the tree house. She hadn't been there long when she saw someone cross the distance from the fence to the tree house. It was a young boy, about four feet tall and very slim, with a full backpack. He cautiously approached the tree house, looked in all directions, and began to climb the ladder. Shannon wished she had thought to bring her camera and remembered she had her phone. She quickly took the phone out and snapped three pictures. Not knowing who this was, she decided to return to the house and discuss the situation with her parents.

After he was out of sight, she quietly found her way back down the path to the house. Mom and Aunt Francie were in the kitchen; Dad was in his office.

"Mom, Dad," she said. "I think I know who has been disturbing the neighborhood."

She brought them up to date on all that had happened that morning and showed them the pictures she had taken on her phone. The first picture was as he started up the ladder and he was looking up. The second was about halfway up, and he was looking away. The last picture was the jackpot. He was looking in Shannon's direction just before he entered the tree house.

"Let me see that," said Aunt Francie. Enlarging the picture, she said, "He looks Hispanic and quite young. Also looks like he hasn't bathed in a while, and he is so thin. I wonder how long he has been living in the tree house."

"Well," said Dad, "the reports of a prowler have dated back a month or so. If he is responsible for those, I am assuming his point of operation has been from there. What I don't know is how he found it. He had to scale a high fence on three sides or access from our backyard. It does give you a start to think this could happen without your knowing anyone was anywhere around. If this had been a grown man, I would be in a panic."

"Yes," said Francie, "but you don't know if there is someone else with him, and, if so, who and where is that person. This boy looks no older than ten, and where are his parents?"

"I want to know if he is alone before deciding what action to take," said Dad. "I don't want to call the police to pick up and scare a young boy unless he is accompanied by an adult. If he is, indeed, alone, I would like to talk to him before calling the authorities."

Mom, although reluctant, and Francie agreed that more information is needed before turning in the trespasser. Francie said, "The sooner you make that decision, the better. This boy looks like he is in need of nutrition and maybe even medical care."

Dad asked Shannon where she hid to observe the boy when he returned. He planned to watch the location for a while before approaching the tree house to make sure there was no one who might look threatening with him.

As thirty-six-year-old Todd settled his five-foot-eleven-inch frame into the hiding place, his sandy blond hair shone in the sunlight, and his bright blue eyes were alert to any movement around him. He wondered how long he would have to remain in this cramped position before seeing their mysterious guest.

Chapter 6

Todd had been in Shannon's hiding place only an hour when he smelled something burning. It looked as though the boy had built a small fire in the tree house, presumably to cook something. This had just become an emergency as a fire in a tree house is a recipe for disaster. Dad approached the tree house and began to cautiously climb the latter. Being careful not to make any noise, he poked his head up just enough to be able to see inside. The young boy was alone, his back to the door, and cooking a piece of meat over an open fire he had made in a metal pan of some sort. Close beside the fire, he glimpsed wilted vegetables—lettuce, broccoli, and carrots. This young boy had apparently been foraging for food. He wondered how he would get into the tree house and get the boy down without setting the tree house on fire.

He felt the ladder shake and looked down. It was Rudy. Rudy motioned for him to come down. Dad slowly descended the ladder.

Rudy said, "Is he alone?"

"Yes," said Dad.

"Let me go up. I can pretend that I am surprised to see anyone in there. Being a kid, it may keep him from panicking."

Dad agreed but told Rudy to be ready to jump down if he became aggressive.

Rudy ascended the ladder and peaked inside. The boy was still cooking his meal, so Rudy stepped on the top rung and said, "Who are you and why are you in my tree house?"

The boy spun around immediately and backed into a corner, tension and fear in his eyes. *"No habla English,"* he said.

"*Y tu habla Espaniol?*" Rudy asked.

He nodded. "*Si.*"

In Rudy's limited Spanish, he asked where he came from and why he was staying in a tree house. It was apparent that the boy did not want to talk, so Rudy said "*Mi nombre Rudy. Su nombre?*"

"*Mi nombre Carlos,*" he said.

The boy relaxed slightly, and Rudy asked if this was the food he had been eating. Again, the response was "*Si.*" Rudy told him his mother had just made lunch and he was welcome to eat with them.

It was obvious the boy was frightened and weighing whether to trust Rudy. He looked at his stash of food and back at Rudy. Eventually, his stomach won the battle, and he nodded.

Descending the ladder, Rudy motioned his dad away so it would not frighten Carlos, at which Todd moved into the hiding place so as not to be seen. Rudy led Carlos out of the woods and to their house. When he entered the back door, he announced that he had brought a friend for lunch. Debra, having known the plan to flush out the trespasser, came around the corner from the kitchen. When she saw that the guest was a boy, she broke into a wide smile.

"*Lo es Carlos. Estas es mi madre,*" Rudy said.

Carlos first noticed that this five-foot-five-inch woman with high cheek bones and dark brown hair had kind brown eyes that crinkled when she smiled.

"You are welcome to join us for lunch," she said.

"Mom, Carlos does not understand English," Rudy explained.

"Oh, sorry." she said. "*Le invitamos a unirse a nostros para el almuerzo.*" Turning to Rudy, she said, "Rudy, you and Carlos get your hands washed, and I will call Dad and Shannon to lunch."

When Todd came in the back door, having crept out of the woods after Rudy and Carlos had gone inside, he asked Debra, "Where is Francie?"

"She had to go downtown to the office. Some concerns with border crime. She will be back for supper," she said.

"Good, I want her to get this whole story. I think this will be a matter for her. This boy is obviously not here legally, and I want to know why he is not with someone who is taking care of him. He looks to be about ten years old. Certainly, not old enough to be taking care of himself. We do not need to question him. It needs to be a professional familiar with the people who are here illegally. We may say something that scares him into running away. For now, we need to keep him here for his safety."

When Shannon came in, Todd and Debra explained the situation and asked her to keep the conversation at lunch light, maybe discussing herself and Rudy, school, whatever, rather than inquiring about him. If he offered information, all the better, but let him lead that conversation. Shannon nodded, indicating that she understood.

Lunch was pleasant with Shannon and Rudy, in their broken Spanish, talking about school and friends while Carlos scarfed down a bowl of potato soup and a turkey sandwich. He was obviously famished. Debra suggested that Rudy and Carlos play some video games, board games, or whatever might interest Carlos and asked Carlos to stay for supper. It was at that point that Carlos seemed to completely relax and actually smiled.

*****

After dinner, Francie announced that the space station was flying over tonight and wondered who wanted to go out and watch it with her. Carlos said that he had never seen it before and would like to watch with her. Shannon and Rudy demurred, saying they had pressing homework.

Sitting on the front porch, waiting for the sighting, Francie asked Carlos, *"Donde estan tus padres?"* (Where are your parents?)

Carlos, ever the strong young boy and not wanting to show weakness, turned away and said nothing.

"Carlos," asked Francie again, *"donde estan tus padres y, donde vives?"* (Where are your parents and where do you live?)

A tear ran down Carlos's cheek, and he said, *"Ellos estan muertos."* (They are dead.)

An hour and a half later, after watching the sighting, Carlos and Francie came inside. Francie asked Carlos if he would stay the night, and they could resume their conversation tomorrow.

Carlos looked at Todd, who nodded and said, "We would love to have him stay. He can sleep in Rudy's room." Walking up the stairs with Carlos, he knocked on Rudy's room and explained that Carlos was spending the night with them. Rudy, whose room was decked out with bunk beds, began to clear away the bottom bed which was always a mess. After Todd returned downstairs, Francie told them what she had learned from Carlos.

"Carlos, his mother Delores and his younger sister Bella left Guatemala over two months ago with a caravan headed to the US. Carlos's father, who was the only breadwinner, had died of an undiagnosed illness. From the description, it could have been COVID-19. Carlos's Uncle Miguel, his mother's brother, on learning of his brother-in-law's death, sent Carlos's mother a message that he had arranged for them to travel with the caravan. He had paid for coyotes to deliver the three of them to the border and then on to El Paso, where he lives," Francie said.

After a long pause, she continued, "Carlos told me that on the trip, coyotes abused the women and children. He told me about a young woman and her aunt whom they met on the trip. Apparently, one of the coyotes killed the aunt and raped the young woman. He said they had threatened to take Bella and even him, but Delores would offer to go with them instead. Were it not for one of the coyotes who befriended Carlos and his family, it would have gone very badly for Delores.

"The trip was very long and very treacherous, which agreed with the accounts that the Border Patrol had heard over and over. They walked for days and days, and those who could not keep up were left behind. Some of the immigrants were so weak by the time they arrived that they died in the desert or drowned in the river. When they reached the Rio Grande, Delores and Bella both got caught in a current and drowned. Carlos tried to save them but could not. Smart boy that he is, when he realized that his mother and sister were dead, he held his breath and dropped below the surface hoping the coyotes would think he had also drowned. It worked. The young coyote who befriended them saw him sink below the surface and pushed him to the bank. He waited until everyone had gone and pulled himself out of the river.”

“Where did they cross the river?” asked Todd.

“Carlos says Del Rio,” said Francie. “And he has somehow made his way here to El Paso in hopes of being united with this uncle.”

“That is a very long trip,” said Todd. “How did he get here?”

“I didn’t push too much,” she said. “I wanted to build some trust with him, so that is a conversation for another day. Needless to say, this young boy has had a very rough time. He has been here for about three weeks, staying in the shadows until he came upon your tree house. He spends his days searching for his uncle and his nights in the tree house.”

“I can only imagine the strength this young boy has, having lost his father, grieving for his mother and sister, and now he cannot find the only family he has left,” said Debra. “But how did he come upon the tree house?”

“Well, you remember those prowler incidents?” Francie said. “Those were Carlos. He would find a house that had a bag of dog food, take a little from the bag, and feed it to the dog so he could rummage in the garbage can for food without the dog barking to alert the household. I told you he is smart. On one of his nightly scavenges in your backyard, he noticed the woods behind your house. Your next-door neighbor let out their dog, which started barking, and Carlos ran into the woods. It was then that he found your tree house. That has been his base of operations since that time.”

“Has he found his uncle?” asked Todd.

“No, he seems to have disappeared. Carlos found the address they had for his uncle, but his landlord was not at home, and the neighbors say they do not know where he is.”

“Does he have a job?” asked Debra.

“Delores had told Carlos that Uncle Miguel works for a meat-packing company, making a good living, but Carlos could not get anyone to tell him which one.”

“So what is our next step?” asked Todd. “Should we contact the police, Border Patrol, what?”

"I would like for Carlos to stay here if it would not be too much of an inconvenience for you, at least until I can locate his uncle. Typically, he should be turned over to the authorities, and, although I know this is not proper protocol, something tells me that Carlos may be in danger, especially since his uncle has disappeared."

"Could you get in trouble for not turning him in?" asked Debra.

"Yes, and I suppose, to a lesser extent, you could, too," said Francie. "It is up to you."

"There is no question that Carlos should stay here until his family can be found and we are sure he is in no danger," said Debra.

Although not an immigration attorney, Todd's legal experience as associate attorney with the Office of City Attorney gave him pause at sidestepping the law on this, but his heart won out, and he nodded in agreement with Debra.

Francie said she would start the search of the local meatpacking plants the next day to try and locate Miguel.

CHAPTER 7

Miguel and his sister, Delores, were born to middle class Mario and Consuela Rameriz in San Antonio de Los Altos, just south of Caracas, Venezuela. Mario worked at an oil refinery until the rise of Hugo Chavez, who effectively shut down the petroleum industry. This precipitated the deterioration of the once wealthy country. Miguel was twenty, and Delores was seventeen when their parents were murdered by the subsequent Maduro regime for protesting the policies that were bankrupting the country and everyone in it, except for the reigning powers. Delores met and fell in love with Quinton Gonzales at one of the protests. She and Quinton married six months later. After their parents' deaths, Miguel and Delores became aware that their lives were in danger because of their political ideology. Delores and Quinton moved to Guatemala, and Miguel made his way to America, where he was granted asylum because his life was in danger from political persecution. He migrated to El Paso, where he was employed by a large meatpacking company.

Delores and Quinton moved to Guatemala in 2013. Quinton went to work at a major textile plant supervising production of yarn. Because of his hard work and loyalty, he was quickly promoted to distribution. They bought a comfortable home in a middle-class neighborhood.

Their first child, Carlos, was born two months later. They were blessed two years later with little Bella. They were a loving, devoted family and lived happily for ten years. Then Quinton became ill. At first, it appeared to be a cold, but after a week, he was no better and continued to get worse. He was admitted to the hospital where he was diagnosed with COVID-19, placed on a ventilator, and succumbed to the illness three days later.

Delores and the children were left with broken hearts and no means of support. She was coming to the end of her rope when a call came from Miguel saying she needed to contact the American embassy for asylum. She called for a hearing the same day. The screening for asylum was not valid as her life was not threatened. Had she not migrated from Venezuela, the claim would have been honored. She explained her situation and that she had family in America and asked about a visa. Again, that was not a valid reason for a visa, and she had no skills so she could apply for a work visa.

She was in despair when she talked with Miguel about the outcome. He told her to be patient; he would get back to her. He called her a week later after talking to an acquaintance who knew someone in the cartel.

"There is a caravan coming to America that will pass through there in a few weeks. You must sell your house and everything except what you can carry." he said. "The cost is $6,000 per person. I will send you the information on how to join and where to send the money."

Delores sold everything, including personal items that they could not carry with them.

"I could only raise $15,000 for the trip," she said when she talked again to Miguel.

"Let me get back to you," he said.

Miguel called his acquaintance and explained the situation. His friend called him back and said that the cartel had agreed to let them join since it was a family unit and the youngest was only eight.

Delores transferred the money according to the directions that Miguel sent her after which instructions were given to her about where to join the caravan.

The number of people waiting to start the trek north was startling. When she saw the crowd of people, Delores regretted what she had done. Selling her home and uprooting the children from their friends was hard enough, but now she was alone in a multitude of strangers with her two young children, who were dependent on her to keep them safe.

Before panic completely took over, a man approached her and called her by name. "José," she queried. "Is that you? Are you traveling with this group?" she asked.

"Yes, Delores, I am," he replied. "I didn't know you were leaving Guatemala. Where is Quinton?"

"Quinton passed away three months ago. Miguel has arranged for this trip, but I had to sell everything we had to pay for the passage," she said. "When did you leave Venezuela?"

"More than two months ago. I was lucky to get out with my life. Are you sure you want to take this trip? It is not easy, in fact, very dangerous, not only from the terrain. But the coyotes who are in charge of the caravan are cruel," he said. "You must watch yourself and your children to make sure you do not stand out for any reason. I am so sorry about Quinton. I hope that you will have a safe passage."

CHAPTER 8

The sea of humanity began their trek on a Monday morning. Although Delores knew that the journey would be difficult, she had some hope now that she would soon be with family again as well as have security for her children and herself.

On the second day of the trip, Delores, Bella, and Carlos found themselves walking with Keisha and Ansa.

Ansa was a five-foot three inch middle-aged Haitian woman with lovely brown eyes, black hair, and a warm smile. Keisha, on the other hand, was a frail, slightly taller, eighteen-year-old Haitian girl with a somber appearance. She had dark brown, almost black eyes set in a beautiful dark complexion with full lips and short dark hair.

Delores introduced herself and the children to Ansa and asked where they were traveling from.

"Brazil," replied Ansa. "I am Ansa, and this is Keisha, my niece. My sister, Elon, still lives in Haiti, but wanted a better life for Keisha. When she heard that I would travel to America, she sent her to travel with me."

"Why did you want to leave your home to travel on such a long journey?" asked Delores.

"After the earthquake in 2010 in Port-Au-Prince, my husband obtained a visa to work in Brazil. There was much construction work there, but in 2016, during the recession, many jobs were eliminated, and he traveled to America where he obtained work. He could not apply to bring me to America because he is there illegally, and I could not apply for asylum. When we heard that the southern border of America was open and that the invitation to come was made by the

American government, he arranged for me to travel with this caravan," said Ansa.

When the caravan stopped for the night, Delores invited Ansa and Keisha to camp with them.

"Do you have family in America?" asked Ansa.

"Yes, my brother, Miguel, lives in Texas. We will live with him. I hope to be able to find work and help him support us," replied Delores.

"Still, if you don't, there are many free things in America. We understand there are charities who will find you a place to live, give you money, and enroll you for services and free health care," said Ansa.

Delores did not respond. She and her family had always worked to pay their way without the thought of seeking aid from others.

The first several days were hard as the group had to walk several miles every day from dawn to dusk, with only breaks to have a bite to eat and relieve themselves. Sanitation was abhorrent but could not be helped. There were no portable potties along the way. The food was sparse as it had to last until the next town where beans and rice and other provisions could be purchased.

They soon entered the Lacandon Jungle and had to cross the Usumacinta River to get to Mexico. Lacandon was known for venomous vipers, monkeys, and jaguars, to name a few of the dangers—not to mention rugged terrain. The din of crying monkeys and jaguars was unsettling, especially for Carlos and Bella.

They crossed the Usamacinta River in boats, twenty to twenty-five migrants in a boat. On the other side, the wealthier migrants were loaded into vehicles and driven to the US southern border. The poorer travelers were destined to walk the remaining 1,270 miles to Eagle Pass, Texas.

The jungle crossing had been brutal. The coyotes pushed them ruthlessly. Those who fell behind were left behind. One woman was bitten by a snake and was left because she became too sick from the bite to continue. It came as a surprise to Delores that none of the guides made an attempt to help her. Those fellow travelers who tried soon saw that they, too, would be abandoned if they slowed down.

There was no way of knowing her fate. The caravan passed deceased bodies as they trekked through the jungle paths—poor souls who were unable or too weak to traverse the jungle paths.

Once they emerged from the jungle, it took a week to cross the Mexican state of Chiapas and would take at least another sixty days to reach the American border. Some of the migrants decided to call it quits and looked for ways to return to their home country.

Delores breathed a sigh of relief now that they had the jungle and the river behind them. But she had seen some disturbing incidents involving some of the coyotes with the women and young girls. Her trepidation began to grow more every day that she and her children were at risk of being abused.

When the group stopped for the night three weeks into the journey, a rough-looking coyote took notice of Keisha. He approached her and told her she could come with him for a while. Ansa stood and asked him to leave her alone whereupon he grabbed Keisha's hand and began to pull her with him. Ansa, following them, grabbed Keisha's hand protesting that he should leave her alone. The coyote back-handed Ansa, knocking her to the pavement. Ansa was bleeding heavily from her head. In the ensuing chaos, the coyote let go of Keisha and disappeared into the crowd that had gathered. A doctor who was traveling with the caravan attempted to help Ansa, but she quickly succumbed to her injuries. The coyotes disposed of her body, they knew not where. Delores quickly gathered Keisha in her arms and comforted her.

The next night, the same man came to Delores's camp, grabbed Keisha and said she could either go with him or she would suffer the same fate has her aunt. Keisha said she was not afraid. He said either she or Bella will come with him. Carlos rose to protect Bella. The coyote knocked him to the ground. Keisha moved between Carlos and the man saying that she would go with him. Delores, torn between protecting her children and coming to the Keisha's defense, demurred asking the coyote to please leave Keisha alone. He laughed at her and dragged Keisha away.

Sometime later that evening, Keisha returned to the camp, obviously in pain and crying. She had been raped and beaten. She sat gingerly apart from the others and would not make eye contact. Delores went to her and, putting her arm around her, said, "I am sorry I could not protect you."

"They raped me and beat me. I am so dirty now."

"You must not let this change who you know you are. This was not your choice, but that of a barbarian. Are you hurt anywhere?" asked Delores.

"My wrist hurt where I was held down, and I am bleeding. I was a virgin, and now I am not worthy of a husband," she cried.

One evening, one of the coyotes visited where Delores, Carlos, Bella, and Keisha were camped. He was a young man, probably in his late teens or early twenties. He talked to Carlos and Bella about where they were from and attempted to talk with Keisha but got no response. In fact, she acted frightened of him. He asked Delores where they were hoping to go in America. Delores was very guarded in her answers, but this young man seemed to be a good person. She introduced herself and the children to him and asked his name.

"Filipe," he responded.

She asked him what led him to this line of work. He responded in a quiet voice that it was his only option. He was forced into service by the cartel. He had been a migrant and was unable to pay the remainder of his fee for passage. His options were to be killed or join the cartel.

"But did you not pay before you began the trip?" Delores asked.

"Si, but I did not have all of the fee for passage, and my relative in America could not raise that and the fee to cross the river when we reached the Rio Grande."

Anxiety began to grow to panic for Delores. She had paid the cartel all of the money she had with the exception of funds for food and necessities during the trip.

"Surely, they cannot kill everyone who cannot come up with more money," she said.

"No, they do not," he said. "If you cannot come up with the extra money, they will need the name of a friend or relative they can contact for the money. If it is not paid, they will give you the option to enter in their sex or labor trade or traffic people and drugs after they cross the border. Young, strong men are forced into service to the cartel, like me. Otherwise, you will be left behind. No one escapes this. It is a long trip, and they will get to everyone in the caravan. I wish I could help you, but I am unable to have any influence on them. I wish you were travelling with a husband. It would be better for you." With sadness in his eyes, he said goodbye to Delores, patted Bella on the head, gave Keisha a sad look, and shook hands with Carlos.

Delores recalled the deal that the cartel had made with her. After she had sold her home and other assets and paid off the mortgage, she had $15,000. The fee was $6,000 per person, but the man she spoke with approved the $15,000 to take the three of them as Bella was only eight years old. It occurred to her that perhaps he was willing to reduce the price knowing that they would extort money from all three of them when they got to the river.

As the weary travelers progressed in their journey, a young boy of perhaps ten years old became very sick. He appeared to be dehydrated from the vomiting and diarrhea. Because no one was treating him, he died. He had been travelling with his father, who became so distraught at the loss of his son that he committed suicide, saying that he had no one left, that if he had not brought them on this trip, his son would still be alive.

Many women and young girls and some of the young boys were raped and beaten by the coyotes. It was said that most of the young girls were given birth control pills by their parents before leaving their homes, knowing they would likely be raped.

CHAPTER 9

Sixteen-year-old Filipe Herrera was not really bad, but a troubled boy. He skirted the law by petty thefts of food and necessities to help his mother, who was abused by his father as was he. Filipe was arrested once but was released by a sympathetic Nicaraguan policeman.

Filipe's mother was a gentle soul who worked by taking in sewing for friends and neighbors. His father was unemployed by choice, depending upon his wife to support his family. Filipe's sister, eighteen-year-old Sara, was a supervisor in a poultry processing plant and helped her mother with the sewing until she married eight months ago. After Sara moved from the home, Filipe's father became even more abusive to him and his mother. Filipe sought friendships from other boys in like circumstances. One such boy was Devante, whose parents had kicked him out of the house for bad behavior. Devante talked of heading to America with one of the caravans to find a job. He encouraged Filipe to come with him, but Filipe, ever loyal to his mother, said he could not leave her with his abusive father.

It was a Saturday night when Filipe's father came home drunk and started beating Filipe's mother. She begged him to stop, and Filipe tried to intervene. The beating was so severe that Filipe feared for his mother's life. In his father's rage, he broke a chair, and, picking up a heavy leg, approached his wife. Filipe, realizing that he intended to kill his mother, picked up a knife and attacked him. As his father fell to the floor, it was clear that he was dead. Filipe's mother began to sob uncontrollably. "You have killed him, Filipe," she sobbed.

"I am sorry, Mother," he said. "He would have killed you."

"My concern is not for him, but for you," his mother said. "You must hide, you must run before I call for help. Filipe, this is my fault. I should have left him years ago. Now, I have made you a criminal."

"But, Mother, this was in defense of you," Filipe said.

"We cannot assume that police will see it that way or even consider that to be an excuse. I will go to Sara and let her know what has happened. You go. Contact her to let her know where you are," she said.

"Mother, I love you. I will go, but I will return or send for you," he said, tears streaming down his face.

Filipe fled the home and went to Devante. He told Devante what had happened, and that he needed to leave. Devante told him that he is planning to join the caravan headed for America tomorrow and urged him to come. Filipe, at last, saw an opportunity to get himself and, ultimately, his mother a better future. One in the free and rich America.

Devante asked him how he would pay the $10,000.

"I will call my sister. Maybe she can raise the money," Filipe said.

Filipe called Sara who said she could only raise $7,000. Devante put Filipe in touch with a cartel member he knew. Devante assured Filipe he could be trusted. After hearing Filipe's story, he agreed to allow him to travel with the understanding that the additional $3,000 would be paid before he would be allowed to cross the border. Filipe called Sara and asked her to contact their cousin who lived in Arizona to raise the additional $3,000 before the caravan reached the border.

With that settled, Filipe was set to travel to America. For the first time in many years, he felt a sense of optimism that his and his mother's future would be better.

The trip was very difficult with hard terrain and truly evil men who took advantage of the women and even children along the way. He witnessed beatings and rapes. The men in the caravan were frightened to come to the aid of the women and children as these animals would kill at the least provocation.

As the caravan came closer to the American border, one of the coyotes came to Filipe. "Your cousin could not raise the $3,000 that you still owe," he said. "The cartel is not happy with that news. We do not take anyone to the border for free."

"But I have already paid $7,000 at the beginning," Filipe replied. "I can get a job once I am in America and pay the rest if we can work out a plan."

"That is not what we agreed upon," the coyote responded. "You will be left in Mexico unless you can be of service to the cartel. There are a few ways that you can work off the remaining balance. And let me warn you, being left in Mexico is not an option if you value your life."

"How can I work off the balance with the cartel?" asked a frightened Filipe.

"Someone will be in touch with you soon," he said.

Devante, hearing the exchange between the coyote and Filipe, approached Filipe cautiously, hoping not be observed by the coyotes. "I overheard your conversation. There are many in the caravan who are in the same position. They are allowing them to work off the balance by working for the cartel."

"How could I do that?" asked Filipe.

"Young, strong men are forced to join the cartel making the trip with the caravans," Devante answered. "Others are made to carry drugs across the border or serve in the sex trade."

❧

CHAPTER 10

After a long, dangerous and difficult trip, the caravan approached the Rio Grande in the Del Rio sector. A man named Rafael demanded $6,000 more for them to cross the river and $2,000 for Keisha. Delores said she had given them all she had. He told her to contact someone to get the money before they would be allowed to cross and gave her his phone to make the call. Delores called Miguel and explained their problem and also told him about Keisha, who has an uncle in America, but does not know how to reach him. Miguel said he would get the money for Delores, Bella, and Carlos and he would try to raise the money for Keisha. Rafael took the phone, getting his name and address, he told him he should transfer the money now.

"I will transfer the money as soon as my family is safely across the river," replied Miguel.

"We can leave them here if you like. It will not go well for them," said Rafael.

"If that is what you want, but I would think $8,000 is better than nothing which is what you will get if you do leave them there," Miguel countered.

"Be assured, it will not go well for you if the money is not paid," said Rafael.

"Understood," said Miguel.

Delores and Bella were both exhausted, and Carlos tried his best to help them into the river. As they neared the center of the river, a baby whose mother was walking with the group was swept from its mother's arm. Bella, trying to get to the baby, was overcome by the current. Reaching for Bella, Delores lost her footing. Delores and Bella both went under. Carlos tried to come to their aid but was pushed away by Filipe who had volunteered to monitor their crossing. Filipe pushed Carlos toward the bank and left him. Quickly, his feet *gaining purchase* on the riverbed, he hurried to find Delores, Bella, and Keisha who were losing ground. Delores had Bella by the hand and was struggling to keep both of them above the surface. Filipe grabbed Delores and swept her toward the bank with Bella in tow. He then grabbed Keisha's hand and shoved her onto the bank. Moving back to the river, he quickly realized that he could not save the baby and returned to the bank where he hid them and himself in the weeds, waiting for the rest of the caravan to pass. Delores was trying to revive Bella while keeping her quiet at the same time.

Carlos, thinking his mother and sister dead, lay on the bank sobbing for a time, then crawled up the bank and made his way to Del Rio. Delores was distraught thinking that Carlos had drowned.

"I pushed him to the bank upriver. He should have been able to pull himself up," said Filipe. "We need to get all of you to safety, and then we will start to look for Carlos."

"Filipe," said Delores, "you have put yourself in danger to save us. If you are caught, what will happen to you?"

"I am sure they will kill me," he replied. "But I would rather be dead than to continue to live as I have for the past year, watching the inhumane things that I have seen. My heart breaks to see people treated as they are, and I am powerless to help. And I know that these people who are willing to risk all on this trip will not find what they are searching for at the end. They will either be heartbroken or dead."

"You have saved us, Filipe," said Delores. "We would have drowned if not for you, and I know that my brother will help to protect and take care of you for that."

The journey across the arid steppe between the Rio Grande River and a point where they could cross into the US was filled with desert shrub and clusters of poplar and asper trees. They were careful to ration their water, knowing that there would be no water until they reached a ranch where they could replenish their bottles.

Delores caught sight of someone lying on the ground just off the trail that they were using. Filipe told her not to go near him.

"But what if he needs help?" she asked.

"If he is not already dead and you help him, he will probably kill you for your water and whatever other provisions you have. He is more likely a drug mule who has died from an accidental overdose. Just being downwind from him could cause you to overdose," he said.

"But only if I take the drug," responded Delores.

"Oh, no! Just touching or inhaling this fentanyl can kill a person. You would be exposing, not only yourself, but Bella and Keisha as well," he explained. "I know how hard it is for you, but you cannot save them."

As they approached a small clump of shrub, Delores spotted a shoe under the vegetation. She heard a small child sobbing. She bent to look under the shrub and was shocked to see a young boy, probably three years old, sitting beside a girl who appeared to be eight or so, lying in the dirt. It was obvious to Delores that she had been raped. On trying to wake up the girl, Delores realized she was dead. Her water bottle was almost empty and had been placed beside the little boy. Delores gathered the little boy in her arms and allowed him to cry into her shoulder. Eventually, when his sobbing had ebbed, she asked if the girl is his sister. He nodded yes. She asked where their parents were, and he showed her a note that had been pinned to his shirt. It contained a phone number to call once he was across the border. Delores asked him where the people were who brought them here. He said, "Gone."

"They are sent by their parents with the coyotes," said Filipe.

"Do they come alone?" asked Delores

"Yes, many do," said Filipe. "They are dependent on the coyotes to bring them over the border where one of the charities is to get them to their destination. Many are raped and left behind. Any who cannot keep up on the journey are left to die along the way. For those who survive the trip, some never make it to Border Patrol or the charity. The cartel uses them in the slave trade or an organ donor business. The little boy is fortunate he is alive, or maybe not. He will probably not survive."

"What shall we do with these children?" asked Delores. "The little girl obviously sacrificed herself to save her brother. We cannot just leave her here."

"That is exactly what we must do," said Filipe. "And we must leave the little boy as well."

"Filipe!" exclaimed Delores. "We cannot leave him. He will die."

"We cannot take him with us, Delores," said Filipe. "We will be lucky to escape with our lives. We can leave him some of our water, but that will only delay what will happen."

"Filipe, if that were Carlos or Bella, I would hope some kind soul would rescue them. Right now, my son is out there somewhere, and I can only hope he is safe. I do not know how we will be able to take care of him, but I do know I cannot leave this child here," said Delores.

They continued walking until they came to Interstate 10. Skirting the usually travelled trails, they crossed at an overpass and went through a fence into a pasture with a barn. Filipe guided them to the structure and, being careful to make sure there was no one in the barn, instructed Delores and the girls to go inside and hide in the hay. He cautioned Delores to keep the baby quiet. Spotting a watering trough, he knew there would be running water and quickly took all of their water bottles. Staying low so as not to attract attention, he came upon the body of a man who had died of stab wounds. He quickly filled the bottles and returned to the barn, constantly checking his surroundings for other migrants or the cartel.

"Can we stay here to rest for a while?" asked Delores. "Keisha and the children are so tired."

As the sun was beginning to set, Filipe reasoned that no one would be coming to the barn tonight.

"Yes, we can stay here tonight, but we must leave before sunrise in the morning," he replied. "The ranch owner will be out early to put out feed and water if this is still a functioning ranch, and there is also the possibility that other people who have crossed into the country may seek shelter here."

They shared what small amount of food they had left from the trip. Filipe knew that he would be responsible for obtaining food although he had little money and no hope of earning any now that he would be on the "hunted" list of the cartel.

They all slept soundly through the night. Even the boy hardly made a sound. When Filipe awakened them, he hastened them to gather their things and follow him. He had not seen or heard anyone but was anxious to get off the property before daylight.

CHAPTER 11

Miguel had contacted his neighbors about raising the money to bring his family across the Rio Grande. Some of his neighbors were able to lend him a small amount of money, and one suggested he ask his employer for a loan against his future earnings. His employer had an employee assistant program from which they could loan or grant money to workers depending upon the reason. He arranged to borrow as much as was allowed without giving a reason. The most he was able to raise was $5,000. He planned to pay that up front and make arrangements to pay the remainder in installments.

José, seeing Delores and Bella sink below the surface of the river, was certain they and Carlos had all perished. Once he was across the river, he called Miguel to tell him the sad news. Miguel, sick with grief for his sister and his niece and nephew, shared the bad news with his neighbors. One of his neighbors, having had personal experience with the cartels as one of his family members came to America as an illegal immigrant, cautioned Miguel that the coyotes were ruthless and to be careful.

When Rafael called to give him transfer information, Miguel told him he was only obligated to pay for safe passage. "I have been notified that they all perished in the river, including the Haitian girl whose aunt was murdered on the trip," he said.

"The cartel will collect this money or else," Rafael replied.

"What do you mean by 'or else'?" asked Miguel.

"You can either serve the cartel by trafficking immigrants or drugs, or they will take it in blood," said Rafael.

"You were given $15,000 up front for the trip, which we understood would bring them to America," Miguel said. "Then to demand additional money to bring them across the river in which you allowed them to drown, how is that fair?"

"We don't do 'fair'," said Rafael. "We do business, and it is my business to collect the balance. And let me be clear, the cartel is rich and would not miss $8,000. But forgiving you would be a bad example to others who may be thinking about not paying. We allowed you time to get the money and started the trip across the river before it was transferred because you gave your word to pay."

"Rafael, I am heartbroken by the loss of my family, but I do not hold the cartel responsible for their deaths. I would never speak of the financial arrangements we made," said Miguel.

"Miguel," replied Rafael, "not only do we not do 'fair', we don't do sympathy and forgiveness either. We expect the $8,000 immediately."

"I will send it as soon as I can make the arrangements," said Miguel.

Miguel, distraught at the loss of his only family and fearful for his life, confided in his neighbor and his landlord, Frank. "If I had not insisted that my sister and her children come to America with the caravan, they would still be alive. Now the cartel has made threats. They will not see reason," Miguel told them.

"These are dangerous men, Miguel," his friend told him.

"If you will not pay the money and you have any place where you can go," said Frank, "you must do it now. And do not let anyone, not even me, know where you are."

As Miguel was adamant he would not pay, he started making plans to fade into the shadows.

❧

CHAPTER 12

From Eagle Pass, Delores, Filipe, Keisha, and the children traveled to Del Rio and then to Sanderson, where Filipe knew some people who would hide them while they started their search for Carlos. They were afraid to turn themselves in to Border Patrol, knowing that would end the search for Carlos, and they feared they would be killed by the cartel if Filipe were recognized. There was no way to know whom they could trust.

None of the contacts that Filipe knew and trusted could offer any information about Carlos. After a few days with no idea where he was, Filipe, Delores, Bella, Keisha, and the boy set out for El Paso to be united with Miguel, hoping that Miguel would have some connections who could help find Carlos.

From Sanderson, they went to Stockton, planning to follow I10 into El Paso. Traveling on foot from Eagle Pass to Stockton had been a long, hot journey. Along the way, it was obvious that Keisha was very weak. Filipe allowed frequent stops to rest and provided as much food as he could, usually by gathering vegetables from gardens along the way or pilfering from fruit stands and convenience stores. Five days into their trek, Keisha became sick, with frequent vomiting and fainting. Filipe, recognizing that she was becoming dehydrated, told Delores and Bella to stay in an abandoned building and took Keisha to the nearest emergency room. Although Keisha had no identification, Filipe knew they would not refuse her care.

Labs were drawn and vital statistics were taken within a few minutes. After a three-hour wait, Keisha was taken to a room. Filipe, who had told the nurse he was Keisha's husband, was allowed to stay with her. The emergency room doctor came a few minutes later and said they would start an IV with fluids to treat her dehydration. He also congratulated Filipe, stating that the lab results show Keisha is very early pregnant. He cautioned that she should take it easy for a while to allow her to regain her strength and prescribed medication for nausea and prenatal vitamins, which were filled by the hospital before they left.

As tears filled Keisha's eyes, Filipe took her hand and said, "*Niña preciosa, no te precoupes. Podemos manejar esto.*" (Precious girl, do not worry. We can handle this.)

After her IV was finished, she was released from the ER.

When Filipe and Keisha rejoined Delores and Bella, Filipe drew Delores aside and told her of the findings in the hospital and said they should remain where they are for a day or two to get Keisha's strength back. The sadness in Delores was palpable. She was heartbroken for Keisha and was desperate to continue their search for Carlos.

"Is there any way we could find transportation part of the way?" she asked Filipe.

"Aside from stealing a car, we could try to hitchhike, but that could be risky. If someone reported us, we would be turned over to DHS or Border Patrol. We also risk running into the cartel. Let me think about it. We all need the rest tonight," he said wearily. "We can talk about it in the morning."

Keisha was feeling better the next morning, having had a good night's sleep and the medication for nausea had helped with the vomiting. They traveled the next two days, and by the time they reached Highway 17, Filipe knew they had to get a ride. The women and the kids could not walk all the way to El Paso, which was a good 175 miles away. They came across a road-side diner, and Filipe knew that they all needed a good meal. They had been living on raw vegetables and canned meat throughout the trip. Filipe still had about $75 in his wallet. He decided to chance buying lunch. Fortunately, they were the only ones in the diner.

They chose a table away from the window and a heavy-set woman with graying hair came out of the kitchen to take their order. "My name's Sadie. What can I get for you?" she asked.

"Do you have a menu?" asked Filipe.

"Sure, hon. Let me get it for you," she said.

Returning with three menus, she said, "Let me know when you're ready to order."

Looking at the items on the menu, they decided that they could all share two meatloaf dinners. That would only cost $20.

"Ma'am," said Filipe.

"Did you see anything you like?" asked Sadie.

"Yes. We would like two meatloaf dinners. And could you bring two extra plates?" asked Filipe. "And we will have water to drink."

"What about the little fella?" asked Sadie.

"He can have part of my dinner," said Delores.

Sadie disappeared, and Delores, Keisha, and the kids were happy to be sitting in comfortable surroundings anticipating a square meal.

When Sadie returned, she had two plates heaping high with meatloaf, mashed potatoes and gravy, and green beans with four rolls, two extra plates, and flatware. "I'll be right back with your drinks, hon," she said.

Filipe and Delores were busy dividing the meals when Sadie returned carrying tea, coffee, and ice water. She also put mac and cheese and chicken fingers in front of the toddler.

"I didn't order that," said Filipe.

"You didn't?" asked Sadie. "Well, I can't return it to the kitchen. Guess that's on me," she said and winked.

Finishing their lunch, Delores, Filipe, and Keisha couldn't remember when their stomachs had been so full and so satiated.

Sadie floated by and asked if everything was okay. "Wonderful," said Delores. "I think you are an angel."

"We need the ticket," said Filipe.

"Got it right here, hon," she said.

"Do you have a phone I could use?" asked Delores. "Our cell phones are dead, and we have not had an opportunity to charge them."

"Sure, hon. Right there in the back," she said, handing the ticket to Filipe.

"There is some mistake," said Filipe. "You only charged us for one meal."

"Sorry, my mistake. Guess that one's on me, too," she said and winked again. "But, you know, I don't see a car out front. You didn't walk here, did you?"

"Yes," said Filipe, "we did."

"Where're you headed?" asked Sadie.

"El Paso," said Filipe.

"Long way on foot," said Sadie. "Don't know how this little fella and your little daughter here can make it on foot. And this young lady," she said laying her hand on Keisha's shoulder, "looks a little peaked."

"We have to make it," said Delores. "My son was lost—" she almost said "crossing the river" and caught herself—"and we think he may be headed to El Paso."

Filipe gave Sadie the money for the bill. When she went to the cash register, Delores said to Filipe, "Miguel is not answering his cell phone, and it does not go to voice mail either. Something is very wrong, I fear."

"You know," said Sadie, returning with the change, "I own this place and been needin' to go to El Paso to pick up some supplies. Today is as good a day as any to go, and there sure ain't no business today. Say, would you like to ride to El Paso with me? There's a motel there in the southern part of the city, reasonable rates, and you guys look like you could use a good night's sleep. I could drop you there. What about it?"

The relief from the adults was obvious when Delores and Keisha both teared up at the same time.

"Let me get my purse," she said, "and we'll be off."

Three hours later, Sadie turned into the parking lot of a motel on Gateway Boulevard. Filipe noted that the nightly rate was $59. He had the girls and the toddler wait outside while he checked in. When he came out, Sadie had waited on him so she could make sure they got to their room okay. Filipe got them all into the room and returned to Sadie.

"I don't know what to say," he said. "No one has ever been this kind to me in my life. I think Delores is right. You must be an angel."

"I recognized that you guys were in bad straits," she said, stuffed a $100 bill into his hand, and promptly got in her car and drove away. But she did look back and noticed in her rearview mirror that she had a tear in her eye.

Filipe suddenly realized how very tired he was.

He had noticed a sign saying there was a fast-food restaurant close, so that evening he walked to the restaurant and bought hamburgers—one for each of them. He even got a milkshake for Bella and the baby to share.

They each took a long shower and then curled up on the soft mattress. Although the two standard beds were crowded, they all slept like babies.

Next morning, Delores said, "Filipe, I would like to find a church and offer thanks to God for bringing us this far and particularly for Sadie. Do you think there is one close by?"

Filipe called the front office and was told that there is a church on Passmore Road, a short walk away. They packed up their things, Filipe checked out, and they set out for St. Patrick Catholic Church. They entered the sanctuary, and Delores, crossing herself, kneeled, and began to pray.

A priest entered the sanctuary and, not recognizing the small group, made his way back to them to welcome them. As he approached them, it was apparent that they were migrants as it appeared they were carrying all of their worldly goods with them.

"Welcome to St. Patrick's," he said. "I am Father Michael. Can I be of service to you?"

Filipe, being wary of anyone they didn't know, simply stated, "No, thank you, Father."

Delores rose and said, "Father, I felt the need to thank God for our good fortune."

"And what good fortune is that, my child?" he asked.

Not knowing what to say, she said, "There is much to be thankful for, Father."

"Would you sit with me for a minute," the priest said and pointed to the pew.

Delores and Filipe sat down while Keisha tended Bella and the boy.

"I see many people," he began, "who come into our church because they have nowhere else to go. We are always open to those in need. Some just need a hot meal and a little while to rest. Others have greater needs. If your family is in need of food or shelter for a short period of time, we are happy to help you."

Filipe sensed that this man could be trusted and said, "Father, we are not all family. Circumstances have brought us together. We have made a long journey. Keisha's aunt was murdered along the way, and we found this young boy alone in the desert, sitting beside his dead sister. Delores and Bella are trying to reunite with her brother who lives here in El Paso."

"And what is your role here, my son?" he asked.

"I have attempted to help them in their journey, acting as their guide," he said.

"Have you had breakfast?" asked Father Michael.

"No, we haven't," said Filipe.

"Come with me. The kitchen is this way," said Father Michael.

While the others were being served, Father Michael asked Filipe to follow him. He took him to his office and, offering him a cup of coffee, asked him to sit down.

"It is obvious to me there is a great need here," he said. "Can you share more of your situation so that we can help?"

Filipe felt led to tell the priest the entire story: the trip from Guatemala; Keisha's being raped and now pregnant by the coyotes who raped her, which he had witnessed in the shadows but was powerless to stop; the river crossing where Carlos became separated from his mother and sister and their happening upon the small boy. He told the priest that he had fallen in love with Keisha and planned to stand by her during her pregnancy but first needed to find Miguel and Carlos.

"Why do you not go to the authorities?" asked Father Michael.

"If the others go to the authorities, they may not be able to continue the search for Carlos," said Filipe.

"But the Border Patrol is releasing immigrants onto the streets of El Paso. They are free to travel as they see fit," the priest countered.

"If Delores, Bella, and Keisha are recognized by the cartel, their lives will be in danger. I suspect that their fee for crossing the river may not have been paid by Miguel as we have been unable to reach his phone. If the cartel is after him, he has probably disappeared."

"How do you know so much about the cartel?" asked Father Michael.

"Because I have been a coyote for over a year now. I have seen things, Father, that I cannot unsee, unspeakable crimes and abuse, even murder. I cannot go back to that. So, you see, I am also in danger of being recognized," said Filipe.

"I see," said Father Michael. "Do you know where Miguel lives?"

"According to Delores, in the Logan Heights area on Lincoln Avenue," he replied.

"I know that area," said the priest. "It is twenty or so miles from here. Now, let's go get you some food while we decide how to proceed"

CHAPTER 13

Todd, Debra, and Francie were enjoying the last few moments of daylight on the front porch. The evening was clear, and there was a chill in the air, signaling that these were the last fleeting days before the weather prohibited an evening chat outside.

"Francie, have you had any luck finding Miguel?" asked Todd.

"No," she replied. "He hasn't been to work in three weeks, and the family from whom he rented a room have not seen him either. I talked with the neighbors, and no one will admit to knowing where he is or why he disappeared. I have contacted all of the hotels and motels in El Paso, and there is no one registered by the name of Miguel Rameriz."

"Which tells you that he is either using an alias or has left the area," said Todd.

"Correct," said Francie. "I left my name and phone number with everyone and asked them to contact me if they hear from him. I emphasized that we are afraid that he may be in some sort of trouble."

Carlos, who had been listening behind the screen door, came out and started down the steps.

"Carlos, where are you going?" asked Debra.

"I am going look for my uncle," he said.

"Carlos," said Francie, "you must be patient. Finding your uncle is like looking for a needle in a haystack. It would be easy if he were not trying to avoid being found. His neighbors, landlord, and employer all say that he just disappeared. Something or someone must have frightened him enough for him to be using an assumed name wherever he is. Was he in any trouble as far as you know?"

"No, and I can't just sit around waiting for you to find him. I must help to look for him," replied Carlos.

"Where would you begin the search?" asked Francie. "I know you were looking for him before we found you in the tree house. Did you have any leads or any clues as to where he may have gone?"

"I went to the apartment where he was renting a room from Mr. Johnson, but he was not home. One of his neighbors said that Uncle Miguel went to work one morning and never came back home," said Carlos. "What do you think could have happened to him?"

"You said your mother gave the coyotes his phone number to call about the money to cross the river," she said pensively. "You also said they allowed you to cross the river. That would tell me that there was no problem with the money. But then something may have happened to change that when you and your family did not complete the crossing. Could he have refused to pay the fee?"

What she did not say to Carlos was that, if that were the case, he could be hiding behind an assumed name because he had either been pressed into an illegal operation or he was dead.

"I don't know whether he paid the fee. The coyotes were to collect it after we crossed the river," he said.

"That is unusual," Francie said, almost to herself. "They always want the money up front."

"Carlos," she continued, "if your uncle has disappeared under a different name, that means he may be in some kind of trouble. You asking around about him could put him and you in danger. Let me handle this. I'll let you know anything that I find out."

"I know how worried you are, Carlos," said Debra, "but Francie has more experience at this type of thing and many more resources."

Carlos, obviously conflicted, went back inside the house but went straight through and out the back door. Disappearing into the woods behind the house, he ran down the trail to the fence beyond the tree house. He climbed the fence and sprinted across the neighbor's backyard to the street. Not wanting to draw attention, he slowed to a walk and headed for the apartment complex where Miguel lived. He climbed to the second floor and knocked on the door to the Johnsons' apartment. He thought perhaps they were not home because it was so long before he heard Mr. Johnson say, "Who is it?"

"It is Carlos, Miguel's nephew," said Carlos.

Mr. Johnson opened the door. "Carlos," said Mr. Johnson with a wild look in his eyes, "you should not be here. The cartel was here yesterday. They are searching for your uncle. They threatened us if we know where he is and do not tell them. I don't think they know that any of his family survived the crossing. They may be watching our home, so please do not come back here for fear you may get us all in trouble."

"But—" Carlos protested.

"No!" said Mr. Johnson, and he closed the door.

Evil eyes were lurking in the dark just below the Johnson apartment. When Carlos came down the stairs, Edwardo stepped out of the darkness and said, "I overheard your conversation with Mr. Johnson. I heard you say that you are Miguel's nephew. I can take you to Miguel. He will be glad to see you."

"Is he safe? I have been searching everywhere, and no one seems to know where he is or why he disappeared," said Carlos.

"He must stay in hiding for now, but I will let him tell you all about it when you see him," said Edwardo. "My car is around the corner."

Carlos, anxious to be reunited with his uncle, climbed into Edwardo's car. The house where Edwardo took Carlos was in a run-down neighborhood and had several cars in the yard.

"Look what I found," announced Edwardo as they entered the house. "Miguel's nephew. He was asking about Miguel at the apartment where Miguel stayed. I'm betting he came up with his mother and sister to the border. There were three of them, and one was a boy."

"Is that right, little man?" asked Jesse, a rough-looking man "Did you cross the river with your family?"

"Yes, but my mother and sister drowned in the river. Where is my uncle?" replied Carlos.

"And how did you survive?" Jesse asked.

"I tried to save them, but I couldn't. I was able to get to the bank," said Carlos. "Where is my uncle?" he repeated.

"That is something that you are going to help us with," said Jesse. "Edwardo, take him down to the basement with the others."

Edwardo pushed Carlos toward the basement door and took him halfway down the stairs to a room where there were at least thirty or more people were being held. Carlos scanned the room, but he did not see Miguel.

"He is not here," said Carlos.

"We know that," said Edwardo. "But he will be once he knows that we have you.'"

It was then that Carlos realized that he had fallen into the very trap that Francie had warned him about. He had been kidnapped as bait to find Uncle Miguel. But what did he do to cause all of this trouble?

Edwardo shoved him the rest of the way down the stairs and disappeared through the door at the top of the stairs. Carlos ran up the stairs and tried to open the door, but it was locked.

Carlos turned to descend the stairs and realized that he was looking at men, women, teenagers, and young children.

"What is this place?" he asked.

"We could not pay to cross the river," said one man sadly, whose wife and small child were clinging to him. "We are being sent to another place to work for the cartel. Some of the children came alone. I overheard the men say they will use them in their sex trade. They have already taken one child and placed her in their 'organ donor program,' whatever that means. This was not what we came all this way for."

As Carlos looked around the room at all of the people, he saw desperation and fear in their faces.

"I am looking for my uncle, Miguel Rameriz. Have you seen him? Maybe they have moved him somewhere else," said Carlos.

"No, but I overheard the men say they were hunting for him. Apparently, he did not pay the crossing fee for his family," said the man.

Carlos's heart sank. He was trapped like the rest of these people, and if they can find Uncle Miguel, they will probably kill him.

CHAPTER 14

"Hey, guys, do you know where Carlos is?" asked Rudy through the front screen.

"He was just here a minute ago," said Debra. "Have you looked in the kitchen?"

"I have looked everywhere. He and I were about to review his language studies, but I cannot find him," Rudy replied.

Todd, Debra, and Francie shared a frantic look. "Francie," said Todd, "are you thinking what I'm thinking?"

"He has slipped out the back door and is looking for Miguel," said Francie. "He could be in grave danger."

"Rudy," said Debra said desperately. "Go check the tree house now and see if he may have gone there."

"Will do," said Rudy.

Rudy rushed out the back door and down the path to the tree house. Climbing the stairs and seeing it empty, he jumped down and ran back to the house.

"He is not there," he said out of breath. "What can we do? I don't know where to look for him," he said.

"I know where to start," said Francie. "Todd, will you go with me to Miguel's house? It is time for the Johnsons to tell us all that they know about Miguel and his disappearance."

"Let me get my keys. I'll meet you at the car," Todd said.

Todd was less concerned about the speed limit than he was about catching up with Carlos before he got to the Johnsons'. Fortune blessed them that the El Paso Police Department was apparently otherwise engaged, and he was not delayed by a traffic stop. When they arrived at the Johnsons' apartment complex, Francie and Todd were careful to peruse the surroundings. Francie noticed a man lurking in the shadows in close proximity to the Johnsons' apartment.

"Stop here and wait a few minutes," she said.

"What's up?" asked Todd.

"I want to see what that guy is up to," she replied. "It looks like he may be watching the Johnsons' apartment. If so, he is probably waiting for Miguel to make contact. He is standing right below the Johnsons'. I am sure he can hear anything they say when they come to the door. So follow my lead."

Todd parked the car, and they climbed the stairs to the Johnsons' front door. When Mr. Johnson came to the door, Francie said, "Are you Frank Johnson?"

Mr. Johnson said "yes" rather reluctantly.

"I am Judy, and this is my husband, Arnold," said Francie, placing her finger over her lips to let him know they were being overheard. "We are members of the church just down the street. Could we come in and meet your wife? We would like to invite your family to visit with us on Sunday."

"Yes," said Frank Johnson, still somewhat reluctantly. "Please come in."

Frank's wife, Kate, who had been in the kitchen, came into the living room, a puzzled look on her face.

"Mr. and Mrs. Johnson," said Francie quietly, "we are sorry to involve you in this issue, but your apartment is being watched. I am with DHS, and we are aware that your tenant, Miguel Rameriz, has disappeared. We need to know why."

Kate said, "Come into the kitchen. I have a pot of coffee going. My name is Kate, and this is my husband, Frank."

Once in the kitchen, she said, "If someone is listening, they can easily hear through the front door."

After Kate served coffee in the kitchen, Todd continued the story, "His nephew, Carlos, has been staying with our family since we found him camping in a tree house on our property. He, his mother, and sister came with one of the caravans. His mother and sister apparently drowned trying to cross the river."

"Carlos has been searching for his uncle since he arrived in El Paso," said Francie. "I have also been searching for Miguel for him, but Carlos has become impatient and disappeared tonight, we assume to look for him. We felt the first place he would come would be to see if you had heard from him. Has Carlos been here tonight?"

Frank said, "Yes, he was here. He told me he was Miguel's nephew, but I told him I do not know where he is."

"Had Carlos been here before tonight?" asked Francie.

"Not that I know of," said Frank. "If so, it would have been when we were not at home."

"What happened with Miguel?" asked Francie.

Frank told Francie and Todd about the cartel notifying Miguel that he needed more money for his family to cross the river and Miguel's attempts to raise the money. "He could only raise part of the money, but then," he said, "someone who knew the family and was traveling in the same caravan called to tell him that his family had all drowned trying to cross. Miguel decided he would not pay the additional money and was threatened by the cartel. He knew he had to disappear."

"Do you know where he is or how to contact him?" asked Todd.

"I do not know where he is, but I do know how to contact him," said Frank.

"We need you to let him know that Carlos is still alive," said Francie. "I am concerned that he may have been abducted from this apartment complex and is in the hands of the cartel who will use him as leverage or even as revenge because Miguel did not pay. I am hoping that Miguel may know where the cartel may be holding him. When you reach him, give him my contact information. I am working outside of the DHS on this case, so he will not be in any trouble. Please be careful in contacting him as I feel sure the cartel will be watching your every move. It is imperative that I speak with him. In the meantime, I will request additional police presence in this area to discourage the cartel."

"I will do as you ask," said Frank.

"Thank you for your help," said Francie. "Now if you will see us the door, we will keep up our cover story."

"It was so nice to meet you both," said Francie as they opened the front door. "Thank you for the coffee, and we hope to see you at church on Sunday."

On their ride back home, Todd asked, "Francie, what makes you think that Carlos has been abducted?"

"We knew within minutes that Carlos was gone. He was on foot, we were in a car. It is a wonder we did not arrive ahead of him at the apartment. Surely, we would have seen him on the street after he left the Johnsons'. You saw the guy watching the Johnsons' apartment? My bet is that they have had surveillance at the Johnsons' ever since Miguel disappeared. Whoever was there when Carlos asked about Miguel probably heard him tell Frank that he is Miguel's nephew. They are waiting now for the Johnsons to contact Miguel and tell him his nephew did not drown, assuming that he will either show up at the apartment or contact the cartel to negotiate Carlos's release. The problem is that the cartel will not release Carlos and will exact revenge on Miguel as well. These people do not play!"

"What I am hearing you say is that Carlos and Miguel are both dead regardless," said Todd.

"Miguel, yes. Carlos, no, but he will probably wish he were," replied Francie.

"In that case, Francie," said Todd, "I want to bring Johnny, my friend in the police department, in on this. We may need some help if we encounter the cartel during our search. We can use him only in the event we feel there is danger, and I would rather the local police department be involved instead of the Border Patrol or DHS. He need not know that Carlos is here illegally."

"I actually think that is a good idea, Todd," said Francie.

*****

No one in the Parker household was able to sleep that night knowing that Carlos might be in the hands of the cartel. Todd and Francie worked late into the night devising a plan to cover as much territory in El Paso as quickly as possible in hopes of finding some clue as to where Carlos might be. Todd planned to drive the streets of El Paso, hoping to get a glimpse of Carlos or maybe discover any suspicious activity. Francie was hoping that Frank could get in touch with Miguel. She hoped that they had impressed the urgency upon him.

"I plan to go back to his employer today and do a deep dive into his employment record as well as talk to some of his coworkers," said Francie. "I hope Frank will have gotten in touch with him and Miguel will call me. Even if he has left the area, a call from him will give us a game plan to find Carlos."

"I'll drive down to Tornado Bus Station on Paisana Drive," said Todd. "I'll also cruise the streets outside the Border Patrol Holding Center and the Annunciation House. Maybe Carlos escaped whoever may have overheard him, and he is hiding in these groups of people. Miguel may even be trying to blend in there. And I know these facilities have grown to capacity and are putting people out on the street. I would not know Miguel if I saw him."

"His employment record will have a picture of him," said Francie. "I will text it to you as soon as I get there, but he may have left El Paso altogether. He thinks his whole family is dead, and his safety has been threatened. He may feel there is nothing to keep him tied to El Paso now."

Todd said, "I thought about that. I just hope that's not the case. We really need to reunite Carlos with him."

"Well," said Todd. "I think we have a strategy. We should try to get some sleep."

CHAPTER 15

The basement was overflowing with humanity when Carlos arrived, but soon it would not be so crowded as the ruthless cartel members came down to retrieve specific women and children, leaving the men mostly behind. On one trip down the stairs, a particularly evil-looking man grabbed a girl around Carlos's age, stripping her from her mother's grasp. Her mother, protesting and begging him not to take her, was knocked to the ground. The child's cries could be heard as it was apparent that she was being mistreated, raped, or who knows what. She was later brought back downstairs, having been beaten and raped. Tears welled up in Carlos's eyes as he remembered what had happened to Keisha, and his compassion for this little girl was overwhelming, but he was powerless to help her or her mother. The men who witnessed this were also frightened to step forward and defend them. After the man went back upstairs, Carlos asked a fellow prisoner next to him what was to happen to them.

"The women and girls will be sold for sex, most of them," he explained. "We will either be sent for slave labor and placed in jobs that will hire illegals. They pay us, we pay the cartel. Some people are here because their country has paid the cartel to bring them here to earn money to send back to their home country. Some of us, if we are not deemed employable, will either have to serve the cartel or we will be executed. Where are your parents? Did you come alone?"

"No, I was separated from my mother and sister in the river. They drowned, but a kind coyote shoved me up on the bank and then tried to rescue my family," Carlos told him.

"It is a tragedy what is happening to us as we travel here. Then only to find that we are worse off than we were in our own country," the man said sadly.

"Yes, if we had stayed in our country, my mother could have done menial jobs, and I could have found work," said Carlos. "As it is, I have lost everything, and the uncle we were coming here to live with has disappeared."

The man looked sadly at Carlos. "How old are you, son?" he asked.

"Ten," answered Carlos.

"So young," he said. "I am sorry."

There was nothing left to say.

As Carlos watched the mother try to comfort her daughter, he overheard the girl whisper to her mother, "Mother, they are planning to kill a lot of people. I heard one of them talking about a powder and how they could kill a lot of people at one time. They didn't know I was listening."

"Shh," her mother said. "You must not let anyone know that you heard anything," she said, hugging her close, tears streaming down her face.

One of the coyotes came down the stairs and started to separate out some of the younger women and girls. They also separated a few of the young boys. As he herded them up the stairs, Carlos could hear the men upstairs talking. One of them said "airborne," and he also heard "stadium" before the door was closed. He looked around and realized that the people left in the basement were older men, a few young men, and himself. There were also older women, among them, the mother of the girl who was raped and who was distraught that her daughter was taken.

"Where are they taking them?" Carlos asked the man beside him.

"They will be sold as sex slaves. The women left here will become laborers, as will we, if they do not kill us. Some of the young, strong men will be pressed into service for the cartel. Why you were not taken, I do not know. You are too young to be a coyote and not the right age for the labor pool."

"They are using me as bait to get my uncle," said Carlos. "We think he could not raise the rest of the money for our crossing, and they are looking for him. Maybe he will come and arrange to work for them if he does not bring the money."

"No," said the man. "They will kill him…very slowly." He did not volunteer that they would probably kill Carlos first, making Miguel watch. That is why he had not been taken.

"But if he offers to work for them in exchange for the money he owes, why would they not let him do that?" asked Carlos.

"The money is not the issue for them. They will make a point not to cross the cartel," said the man.

Fear which soon became panic began to rise in Carlos.

Through a window in the basement, they could hear those who had been taken crying and shrieking as they were being loaded into a van and driven away.

Carlos waited with dreaded anticipation to hear footsteps at the top of the stairs. After a while, when no one came, he heard heated voices. He quietly started ascending the stairs to the objections of the man who he had been talking with. As he reached the top step, he could clearly hear the conversation in the front room.

"You said you knew someone who could handle this job," said one of the men.

"They will be here. I just talked with Ross. They have had a run-in with a rival gang, but they will still be here in time to place the package before the game starts," said another man.

"This had better go off as planned," said the first man.

Carlos quickly descended the stairs and wondered what all of that meant but was certain it was connected to what the young girl had whispered to her mother.

CHAPTER 16

Father Michael closed the door to his study and entered a phone number into his cell. "Ronaldo," he said, "can you come by my office today? I have something I need you to do for me."

Later that morning, Ronaldo strolled into Father Michael's office and, accepting a cup of tea, sat down. "Father Michael," he said, "what do you need from me?"

"Ronaldo, this is very sensitive," said Father Michael. "I have a group of what I assume are illegal immigrants who have come a long way to find a brother who may be missing. Apparently, the brother is legal here, but for some reason has apparently disappeared as his sister cannot reach his cell phone. He may not know that his sister is alive and looking for him. The sister was also separated from her son trying to cross the river. We assume he is alive, but he may not know that his mother and sister survived the crossing."

"How tragic," said Ronaldo.

"The young man who has been traveling with them has given me the general location where the uncle was living before he disappeared. I know you are good at keeping a low profile while locating people who don't want to be found. I would like for you to travel to Logan Heights and see if you can locate the apartment on Lincoln Avenue where he lived. You must be very careful not to let anyone know who you are looking for as, if he is in trouble with the cartel, they will probably be watching his residence."

"And once we find him, what do we do with him?" asked Ronaldo.

"Let him know that his sister is looking for him, but do not bring him to the church. It could reveal our location to the cartel, compromising those we are obligated to protect," Father Michael said.

"I will find Miguel, Father, and I will be discreet," said Ronaldo as he left by the side door.

Father Michael picked up the phone and dialed Sister Janice. "Would you come to my office, Sister Janice?" he said.

After meeting with Sister Janice, Father Michael went back to the kitchen where Filipe and the others were lingering over breakfast.

"Did you get enough to eat?" Father Michael asked the travelers.

"Everything was wonderful," said Delores.

"Now that you have refreshed yourselves, I will have Sister Janice show you to some rooms where you can stay until you are ready to continue your journey," he said.

"But, Father," protested Delores, "we must be on our way to find my brother."

"My child," said Father Michael, "you must be patient. I have someone looking into your brother's whereabouts. Give us until tomorrow before you decide whether to leave. In the meantime, Sister Janice will see that you are comfortable."

Filipe stood and said to Delores, "We still have twenty miles to go. A day of rest and a good night's sleep will be good for us."

Delores acquiesced, and Sister Janice asked the group to follow her. She led them to one room for Delores, Bella, and the boy, one for Filipe, and the third for Keisha. She followed Keisha into her room and said, "Father Michael tells me that you are pregnant, my child."

"Yes, Sister," said Keisha. "I was raped on the trip to the border. The baby will belong to one of the men who raped me."

"There were more than one?" she asked.

"There were three," Keisha said, beginning to sob.

"At the same time?" Sister Janice asked.

"Yes," said Keisha.

"I will ask Father Michael to make arrangements for a doctor to see you," said Sister Janice. "You must be checked for sexually transmitted diseases."

"I plan to have an abortion even though it is against my religious upbringing," sobbed Keisha.

Sister Janice moved to put her arm around Keisha's shoulders, "God would not have allowed you to become pregnant if He did not have a plan for the child. You must talk with Father Michael before you make such a decision. For now, you must rest. Your journey has been long and traumatic. We will help you to recover physically and spiritually."

Sister Janice reported her conversation with Keisha to Father Michael.

At the end of the day, they all, having finished dinner, headed for their rooms.

"Keisha," said Father Michael. "Could I have a word with you?"

"Yes, Father," she said, following him to his study.

"Keisha," he said, pouring her a cup of tea. "Sister Janice tells me that you do not plan to have your baby. Is that true?"

"Father, under normal circumstances, I would not consider abortion as it is against my faith and all that I have been raised to believe," she said. "But this is not a normal circumstance, which I am sure Sister Janice told you. If I had this baby, every time I looked at it, I would relive that horrible two hours all over again. I don't even know whose it is. How can I have this child?"

"My child, many children are adopted by couples who do not know who the father, and many times, even the mother are," he responded. "But I understand that what you went through is unspeakable. Yet our God and Father is the healer of all things. He will take you through the valley and bring you out on the other side."

"How," she asked, "would I be able to provide for a baby? I have no family. My aunt was murdered by a coyote. My only other relative is my mother, who is still in Haiti living in terrible conditions, and an uncle who I don't even know how to reach. No, there is no way I can take care of a child."

"And yet there is one here in this very building who loves you enough to take on the responsibility for you and another man's child," said Father Michael.

"Who can that be?" asked Keisha.

"Filipe," said Father Michael. "While he may not have declared his love for you, he has pledged to me that he will stand by you no matter what. That is love as Christ loves us. You need not make a decision right now, but I ask you to pray about this and talk to me after you have decided what you have been led to do."

As the shadows were falling across the façade of the church, Ronaldo returned. "I have found where Miguel was living," he told Father Michael. "He was renting a room from a Frank Johnson in Apt 2D of the Lincoln Apartments. As I approached the apartment building, I noticed a man watching the apartment. I thought it best to let you decide how we should proceed."

"Yes, I was afraid of that," said the father. "Did you get his phone number?"

"Of course, Father," said Ronaldo.

Father Michael entered the number in his cell phone.

"Hello," answered Mrs. Johnson.

"Hello," said Father Michael. "Is this the residence of Frank Johnson?"

"Yes, it is," said Mrs. Johnson.

"May I speak with Frank? This is Father Michael of St. Patrick Catholic Church."

"Hello," Frank answered, rather guardedly.

"Mr. Johnson, I am Father Michael of St. Patrick Catholic Church. I have information concerning family members of Miguel Rameriz whom I believe you know," he said.

"I know about his nephew," said Frank. "He has been here already."

"Praise be to God," said Father Michael. "Then he is alive. But I have news of his sister and his niece. They did survive the trip and are anxious to reunite with him, but we understand that he is no longer there. Can you help us to find him?"

"Father, he is in much trouble with the cartel," said Frank. "They are watching our apartment around the clock waiting for him to return, and I fear for the safety of his nephew."

"I understand," said Father. "If you can reach him, let him know that his family is safe and being cared for until we can work this out."

CHAPTER 17

Todd and Francie went their separate ways the next morning. Francie went to meet with Miguel's employer. Todd drove down to the bus station, scanning both sides of the street as he went. The traffic across the border had become so bad that the NGOs and DHS could not house all of the migrants. They were being released into the city of El Paso and camping along the streets, making it more challenging to recognize Carlos if he were intermingled with the other migrants. The bus station was completely full and overflowing, but Carlos was not there. Todd visited some of the shelters, but Carlos was nowhere to be found. He began to cruise the streets, looking for any place where the cartel may have taken Carlos.

Meanwhile, Francie arrived at Miguel's employer. She asked for the manager. When she was told he was not available, she flashed her badge, which was incredibly helpful in getting her into the manager's office.

"We only hire legals here," he immediately said antagonistically.

"Not interested," Francie said, noting that his name tag said Allen Moore. "What I am interested in is one of your employees who has disappeared. Miguel Rameriz. He apparently had family coming up with one of the groups of migrants. He may have been asked for additional money to get them over the river and refused because he was told they had all perished in the river. Turns out his nephew survived the crossing and is looking for him. I need any help you can give me to find him as his life and that of his nephew are in danger. Did he have any wages due him?"

His demeanor instantly changed, and he said, "Well, Miguel is here on a work visa and working toward his citizenship. But no, he has no wages due. He borrowed $5,000 before he disappeared. We do not require an explanation for the loan at that level. What else can I provide to you that may be helpful?" he asked.

"Can you think of anywhere he may have gone to hide? We are concerned that he may have left the area completely thinking that his entire family is dead," she said. "Is there anything in his employment file that might help us?"

"Let me look at his personnel file and see who his emergency contact is," he said. "Maybe that will give us a place to start."

Francie said, "I really appreciate your help."

"Well, it says here that we are to contact his landlord, Frank Johnson, or secondarily a Jane Elliott. I have her telephone number if you want it," he said.

Francie thanked him and turned to leave. She paused and, turning to him, said, "Mr. Moore, would you give me a copy of his picture ID, and has anyone else inquired about Miguel?"

"I believe a man came to our front desk shortly after he went missing asking about him. I was not here," he explained.

"Do you know what information he was given?" Francie asked.

"None, no one knows where he is, and there was no way to get to his personnel file as I have the only access to the files," he replied.

"Thank you, Mr. Moore," she said and answered an incoming call as she left the building.

She texted Miguel's picture to Todd before she put the key in her car door.

Todd was slowly driving into a particularly depressed street in El Paso when his phone rang. "Hello, Francie," he said. "I've struck out so far."

"Well, I have some news," she said. "Frank Johnson called me. Miguel's sister and niece are alive and staying at a church here in El Paso. The priest from the church called him. I asked if he had contacted Miguel yet, and he said no, that he wanted to call me first. I told him to wait until I get back with him."

"I think that is wise—" he paused as he slowly came to a stop. "Francie, I am looking at a house with a white van parked out front. There are several women and girls being put in the van, and it looks like it is against their will. Do you think this could be a stash house for the cartel?"

"It sure sounds like it," she said. "Get your friend from the police department on the phone and tell him to follow the van and give us a position. I will get Border Patrol there as soon as possible. If El Paso police takes down the people in the house and Carlos is there, we may be able to extract him before Border Patrol gets there."

Todd immediately called Johnny Cooper and brought him up to speed. Johnny dispatched units to locate and follow the van and three units and the SWAT team to the stash house and put the pedal to the metal to get there himself.

SWAT breached the house and arrested the cartel monsters while the police searched the rest of the house. The migrants in the basement, hearing the commotion upstairs, began to bang on the basement walls, and one came up the stairs to the door. The police broke down the basement door. Seeing the fifteen or more people, they called for transport and started leading the migrants upstairs. Todd followed Johnny into the house and, seeing Carlos, motioned him over to him. Johnny got both of them out of the house and into Todd's car. He left immediately for the precinct.

In the meantime, Border Patrol had apprehended the white van and arrested the driver, charging him with human trafficking. He turned out to be a teenager recruited by the cartel. The migrants were taken to a local church for temporary shelter.

When Carlos got into the car with Todd, he said, "One of the girls in the basement overheard the men talking about killing a lot of people at one time. They mentioned a powder and the word 'stadium.' Then I heard them arguing about someone who was supposed to be here to pick up a package to be placed before a game."

Todd called Francie. "Francie, Carlos has heard that the cartel is planning something involving a lot of people with a powder and a stadium. Could this be powdered fentanyl?"

"Oh, no," she said. "I am headed to the police department now to interrogate the suspects. Did he hear anything about location? If this is an indoor stadium and they can launch it airborne, it could kill thousands. Where is a local stadium big enough for that to happen?"

"Sounds like it is for a game happening soon. There was anger that the package might not get placed before the game starts," said Todd.

"So best guess. What do you think?" asked Francie.

"Cowboy Stadium in Dallas would make a statement," said Todd.

"Todd, if they are planning this sort of attack here, they could be launching attacks across the country. Is that all Carlos knows?" she asked.

"That was all he heard. I'm taking Carlos home with me. I will fill him in on the way. Call me when you know something," Todd said.

"No," she said. "Bring Carlos to the police station. In case we didn't get all of them, we don't want Carlos connected to you and your family. I will talk to Johnny, and I want the FBI here. We can keep him isolated until we can investigate his report. If what he has reported proves to be true, his entire family will be in danger."

"Okay. I'll see you in a few," he said.

Johnny met Todd and Carlos when they arrived and rushed Carlos off to a secure location to wait on the FBI. Todd had told Carlos that his mother and Bella were both safe and that they were still looking for Miguel. Carlos was anxious to see his mother and sister, but Todd told him he would have to be patient. They must make sure that they would be safe before reuniting them.

"Where is Francie?" Todd asked Johnny.

"She is questioning the suspects," Johnny said. "She said you should go home and she will be there when she is finished with the interrogations."

Todd said, "Johnny, thanks for your help getting Carlos back."

"Hopefully, we hit the jackpot with this bust, Todd," Johnny said. "We seized one thousand pounds of powdered fentanyl and ten thousand fentanyl pills. So they are off the street, and we saved lives. Go home and get some rest. You look terrible."

EPILOGUE

Todd had called Debra on his way home to let her know Carlos was safe. When he arrived home, the family were gathered around the kitchen table waiting to hear about how he had found Carlos.

"Honestly, I was about to give up when I came upon a house with a white van in front. Women and young girls and boys were being loaded into the back. The frantic look on their faces along with the urgency of the men herding them was the tip-off," said Todd.

"Was Carlos with them?" asked Shannon.

"No, so I felt that he was still in the house. Knowing they were probably holding him as a lure for Miguel made me pretty sure they would not move him yet," he replied.

"Todd," said Debra frantically, "did you go into that house to get him by yourself?"

"Oh, no, no, no!" he was quick to answer. "I immediately called Francie. She told me to hang back and call Johnny to send police units and SWAT. She called Border Patrol to intercept the van." He described the scene in the house once SWAT went in and how Johnny helped get Carlos out and into Todd's car.

"Cool!" exclaimed Rudy. "My dad is an undercover agent. When the police went in, did they find Miguel?"

"No," he said sadly. "Francie met Border Patrol at the police station to interrogate the smuggler, and I headed there where Johnny met me and got Carlos to a secure location." He told them what he knew about the threat Carlos had overheard. Assuming it would be a long night, Debra put on a pot of coffee for them while they waited for Francie to come home.

Late in the evening, Francie arrived. Debra poured a cup of coffee and set it down at the table for her.

"Where is Carlos, and what do you know about Miguel, Francie?" asked Debra.

"On my way to the police station, I called John and told him what Carlos had said about overhearing plans to use a powder to kill a lot of people at one time," Francie began. "John called the FBI and was told that there had been chatter in Tennessee, Wisconsin, and Los Angeles about a possible release of an airborne substance intended to cause mass casualties. He said, having heard my report, they will open investigations into all fifty states since the cartels has infiltrated so far into the country. I told him that according to what Carlos had said, a gang was going to handle delivering the agent to the venue here. I told him I would call him after I interrogated the persons in the stash house."

"Did you get a confession?" asked Todd.

"We did get one of the younger men who was driving the van to admit to human smuggling," she said. "I told him that if he knows anything about a plan to cause multiple casualties and he does not notify us, he will be held for multiple charges of premeditated murder, and he could be sentenced to death. He was more afraid of what the cartel would do to him than he was with the death penalty. By that time, the FBI arrived. One of their agents and I tag-teamed, questioning the men from the stash house. After the FBI agent offered him witness protection for his testimony, one of the cartel members rolled on the cartel and the gang they had hired. That's the good news. The bad news is the substance is powdered fentanyl. They had planned to introduce it at Cowboy Stadium during the football game this weekend through the ventilation system."

"That is frightening," Todd said. "Think of all of the football games this weekend. They could kill thousands of people."

Francie said, "We just need to pray that the FBI can identify who is planting the drug now that they know where they should be looking. Indoor stadiums will all be scrutinized, but even outdoor stadiums are vulnerable. It could be introduced into the food and beverages among other ways."

"What about Carlos?" asked Shannon.

"Working through Father Michael, Carlos will be reunited with his mother and sister. Frank knows how to reach Miguel. The FBI will pick him up, and all four of them will be relocated and given new identities in exchange for their testimonies," said Francie. "Father Michael also told me that he had just married a young couple who had travelled in the caravan with them. The young man was a coyote and can be valuable in helping to bring down cartel members, so they will also put them in witness protection. And he mentioned a toddler that Delores and the young man rescued while they were crossing the steppe. They called the number that the little boy had on him. Instead of a relative, the guy on the other end of the line turned out to be a sex trafficker. Father Michael has a young couple in his parish who are unable to have children, and they will adopt him. At least, something worked out well."

Debra asked, "Do you think with all of their testimony, it will stop the cartels?"

"Debra," said Francie, "it is a tiny drop in a big bucket, but it is a start. With over one million 'gotaways' in our country right now, we will have to be constantly vigilant. Among those 'gotaways' are probably cartel and gang members as well as hardened criminals and terrorists. Otherwise, they would not have evaded Border Patrol. Homeland will be watching and listening, but no guarantees. Our national security is fragile on any given day, but we are now in a state of heightened risk."

Faces around the table reflected the concern that Francie had just expressed.

"But," said Francie, her face brightening, "I have some good news. The last time I talked to John tonight, he is excited that I am coming home tomorrow, and he is working on setting up a cruise for us. He wants you all to come with us. I never thought I would hear him excited to travel again."

"I believe I can clear my calendar," said Todd. And the faces around the table reflected Francie's excitement.

ABOUT THE AUTHOR

Nina Wolfe is the proud mother of one son and grandmother of three grandchildren. She spent fifty-six years working for a large medical practice, most as the administrator. During those years, she was a frustrated writer, with little time to devote to her passion. Having retired last year, she is thrilled to be able to share this story with her readers. Though it is fiction, the story is based on current day events.

www.ingramcontent.com/pod-product-compliance
Lightning Source LLC
Chambersburg PA
CBHW021128130726
47988CB00003B/1205